MW01148129

THE UNCOMMON CENT'S JOURNEY

BRAD MULLER

RoseDog Books
PITTSBURGH, PENNSYLVANIA 15238

The contents of this work, including, but not limited to, the accuracy of events, people, and places depicted; opinions expressed; permission to use previously published materials included; and any advice given or actions advocated are solely the responsibility of the author, who assumes all liability for said work and indemnifies the publisher against any claims stemming from publication of the work.

All Rights Reserved
Copyright © 2022 by Brad Muller

No part of this book may be reproduced or transmitted, downloaded, distributed, reverse engineered, or stored in or introduced into any information storage and retrieval system, in any form or by any means, including photocopying and recording, whether electronic or mechanical, now known or hereinafter invented without permission in writing from the publisher.

RoseDog Books
585 Alpha Drive
Suite 103
Pittsburgh, PA 15238
Visit our website at *www.rosedogbookstore.com*

ISBN: 978-1-63937-566-0
eISBN: 978-1-63937-606-3

CONTENTS

NOVEMBER 1943

DENVER, CO

Gene dodged the streetcar and stuffed his hands back into his coat pockets to protect them from the bitter winter wind. His left hand fished around for the coin to make sure it was still in his coat pocket. Employment at the Denver Ordinance Plant to help the war effort is the only thing that kept him in the city. As part of the custodial staff, he didn't really have anything to do with what was being made there, but he still felt like he was doing his part. His black skin was an ashy gray in the cold weather. Gene was only fifty-five, but he looked older from a harder life; a trait passed on his from his father and grandfather.

Gene didn't make much money, and his wife, Darlene, had died a few years back. Pneumonia is what the doctors told him. He longed for a time when he could splurge for a night down in Five Points to listen to a band in one of the jazz clubs.

"Maybe Rice's Tap Room next time," Gene said to himself as he thought about tomorrow being pay day and what his needs would be for the next few days. "Perhaps next week."

He always said, "next week," knowing full-well that he wouldn't be going. Gene wouldn't really think of going there without Darlene anyway. That was their special thing. A night out with music and maybe a drink or two. That was in the past. He had other things to take care of now.

He hummed Duke Ellington's "It Don't Mean a Thing" as he walked. Gene always found a way to be cheerful.

However, walking in the cold was never fun. As he crossed over West Colfax Avenue, he knew he still had about a ten-minute trek to get home. The two-bedroom apartment was crowded with his twenty-five-year-old daughter, his son-in-law, and three-month old grandson occupying the larger bedroom. He didn't mind though. He needed the company. Charlotte had married a good man in Bennie, even though he struggled to support his family financially.

There were no automobiles on the street for several blocks now. He pulled his father's pocket watch from the chain attached to his belt. It was after 6 p.m. and already dark. All he could hear was the crunch of the stiff snow under his feet as he walked. The large blanket of unplowed snow seemed to muffle all the sound, except his own breathing. There were no smells either, other than cold snow. Sometimes Gene liked to take a deep breath out in the snow. It smelled clean to him. A cloudless sky allowed him to see his own breath in the moonlight.

Gene needed to pick up the pace. Bennie wouldn't be home from work for another hour, and Charlotte would need to leave soon for her job at the hotel. That meant that he would get to rock little Abraham to sleep tonight. That was the best part of his day. In fact, the only thing that could take the smile off Gene's face was when he thought how unfortunate it was that Darlene never had the chance to hold her grandson.

He noticed his own silent steps once again, enjoying the peacefulness of it all. Gene finally turned the corner and saw the light on in his second story apartment. The rest of the red brick building was dark.

Stomping his feet three times apiece, he shook off all the snow that had collected on his boots and made his way upstairs. The door was unlocked. It always was. The apartment was cold, and Charlotte was gently trying to coax a burp out of Abraham. The radio crackled and played softly from the main room. Fats Waller sang "Ain't Misbehavin'."

"Did I miss dinner?" Gene whispered with a smile.

Charlotte smiled back. She was already dressed for work but had a towel over her shoulder in case Abraham spit up any of his mother's milk.

Gene reached out for his grandson, gently kissing his daughter's cheek at the same time.

"I've got this," he said.

Gene's weathered hands were gentle on Abraham's back. Within seconds a wet belch came forth, as did a small blob of milk on to his un-toweled shoulder. He and Charlotte laughed quietly. Charlotte inherited her father's cheerful demeanor.

Gene walked Abraham over to the white wooden crib in the large bedroom. It was warmer than the rest of the apartment. He skillfully placed the child down in the center of the crib without a sound.

"Thank goodness he's a good sleeper," Gene said to himself, not for the first time. He was convinced that Darlene was still there somehow, having a calming effect on the child as she always did on him. Maybe she was singing a lullaby that only Abraham could hear.

As he turned to walk out, Gene remembered the coin in his pocket and walked to the tiny white piggy bank sitting on the little table next to the crib. He fished out the shiny 1943 D copper penny and held it in between his thumb and middle finger, as if to show it to Abraham.

"This was made right here, about the same time you arrived," Gene whispered. "It's special, just like you. See? This man on the front, his name is Abraham, too. Just like you."

Gene tilted the penny back at himself, noticing the small chip in the 16th president's nose. Most of the pennies made at the Denver mint were made of steel because of the war, but there were a few that were made of copper. Apparently, someone had forgotten to take out all the copper planchets off the press when they started printing them.

"Mr. Thomas told me this is a lucky penny," Gene said. "He got it from a friend who works right there at the mint. He wasn't supposed to take it, but we won't tell anyone right?"

Gene rubbed the chipped coin between his fingers. He was looking at the penny but speaking to the boy.

"I wonder where you will go," Gene said, deftly dropping the penny into the bank. "I wonder where life will take you, and what you will see when you leave here. I hope you'll come back and tell me what your eyes have seen some day."

As Charlotte stood in the doorway, Gene began telling the sleeping child about his grandfather's tales as an escaped slave in South Carolina.

Charlotte left without another word but smiled as she wrapped a scarf around her face, slid on her heavy coat and prepared for her own cold walk into the night.

WOODWARD, OKLAHOMA

Cool air breezed through Ramona's open window. She liked to keep her bedroom cool, so she left a window open quite often. You never knew what the temperature would be like this time of year in the southern plains. You could feel a wintery bite or even summer's warmth within the same month.

Ramona yawned loudly, which amused her. The twenty-year-old hadn't slept well as a strong wind howled most of the night. She could see her father, Orville, already hard at work on their farm. It was after 6 a.m., so he had already milked the cows and was on to other chores.

"Not too much longer," Ramona told herself. "Save a little money, take the train to New York, and make it to Broadway."

Ramona had told herself this every morning. She was a good dancer, maybe the best Woodward had ever seen, but maybe not as good as she thought. She was confident though, and anything was better than the status quo. Despite spending all her life in Woodward, Ramona had never taken to small-town, farm life. Ever since she took her first dance lesson at age six from Miss Taylor in town, she was hooked. She couldn't get enough of Fred and Ginger whenever their latest film was playing in town. She would scrounge up nickels and dimes and watch the same movie over and over. Now she just needed to save enough to get to New York.

Orville didn't make enough money on the farm to send her to college or a proper dance school, so after graduating from high school, Ramona found a job as a telephone operator. It didn't pay much, and she would occasionally wait tables in the café. Woodward wasn't a large town, but larger than some of the surrounding towns. After getting hit hard by the Great Depression, it rebounded nicely during World War II.

Ramona crossed the creaky wood floor into the kitchen, splashed some water on her face, and put on the denim pants and light brown shirt she had just washed, but liked to wear for farm chores. She put on her mother's apron to fix breakfast for Orville and herself. Ramona fixed all the meals since mama passed.

"Cows are spooked about something," Orville announced as he stepped into the kitchen, already covered in a fine layer of dust from his morning chores.

He took his place at the table, and Ramona placed a plate full of bacon and two fried eggs in front of him. Fixing her own plate, she kissed him on the top of his dirty forehead and sat across from her father.

"How much longer is this strike of yours going to go on?" Orville asked.

"Daddy, all the telephone operators around the country are on strike," Ramona said, trying to sound proper. "So, we have to. I'm only going to picket for a little while today, then I'm going to pick up a shift at the diner. Don't worry, I'll earn today."

Orville grumbled something unintelligible as he shoved eggs and bacon into his unshaven face.

"Looks like we got a little rain last night," Ramona said, trying to change the subject. "I've never seen fog like that either."

"Yeah, there's a storm coming I think," Orville said. "It's kind of chilly though, so maybe it's nothing big."

Ramona finished her breakfast, pecked her father's forehead, and went out to do her daily chores without being told. Tanner and Brian, their two field hands, would be in later today to help out. She was a good girl, and although Orville hated the idea of being alone, he wanted her to chase her dreams and be happy.

A few hours later, she washed off the layer of dust, put on her gray skirt and blue shirt, then hopped on her bicycle to take the dirt road three miles into town. Woodward was mostly flat but surrounded by hills. There was an old Native-American legend that the hills protected the town from the terrible storms that were common on the plains. Ramona noticed the weather slowly growing warmer on her ride.

After an hour of picketing with her fellow telephone operators, Ramona snuck away to the café, and nodded to Agnes at the cash register as she grabbed a pencil and notepad, then put on a clean apron. Traffic was light today. Ramona killed time by scanning the headlines in the newspaper that was left behind by a customer. She never really read all of the articles, just the headline and maybe the first paragraph. Henry Ford had just died, and a black man named Jackie Robinson was going to play baseball for the Brooklyn Dodgers.

After an uneventful few hours Ramona went back to the picket line. She and her co-workers would fill-in for each other throughout the day. Many of her colleagues believed they were doing something important. Some, like Ramona, didn't want to be ostracized, so they did as they were told. This gave Ramona plenty of time to daydream about Broadway. Two coworkers were actually manning the lines inside. They answered anyone's attempt at a phone call but told the voice on the other end that they were only patching through emergency calls.

At half past five, Ramona mounted her bicycle and started to pedal home. It was much warmer at the end of the day than it should have been. She went past the Woodward Theater where Ingrid Bergman was starring in *Rage in Heaven.*

"Not my kind of movie," Ramona thought to herself.

When she knew she was out of everyone's ear shot, she began to belt out "Singing in the Rain" as drops began to fall upon her own head. She didn't have an umbrella, but she didn't care. In her mind, she was on Broadway, and she was hitting all the right notes.

By the time she got home, she was surprised to find that Orville was already making preparations for dinner. Leigh-Ann Jenkins, their closest neighbor about a quarter mile away from the back of the farmhouse, was there with her six-year-old girl, June.

"Well, isn't this a surprise!" Ramona exclaimed.

"Ms. Jenkins had a couple of horses get loose today and her field hands were off," Orville explained. "So, she came over, and I sent Tanner and Brian over there to track 'em down. Looks like her animals are acting a bit queer today, too. I figured since she walked all the way over here and this rain is coming in, we could all eat supper together."

Farmers helped each other. Nobody had a lot extra to provide, but Orville lived by the rule that what goes around, comes around. Besides, he wasn't going to send a woman and child into a storm.

Ramona walked over to take over the cooking duties, but Leigh-Ann stopped her and sidled up next to Orville.

"We've got this," Leigh-Ann said. "Why don't you play with June?"

The little girl popped up off the floor, giggled, and with her Raggedy Anne doll in hand, she pulled Ramona toward the porch. Ramona didn't mind. She knew Orville was lonely, and Leigh-Ann was a widow who was close to his age. Some company would be nice.

The increased humidity felt odd to Ramona, but she was quickly distracted by her tiny visitor. Ramona and June chased each other, while the little girl would randomly veer off to chase one of the chickens. Ramona was thankful for the occasional break.

Ramona was petting Nanny, one of their two cows, when June sauntered over to the barn.

"Miss Ramona," the child asked. "Can I give you a present?"

"A present for me?" Ramona played along. "It's not my birthday. What do you want to give me?"

June reached into the front pocket of her dress, pulling out a piece of hard candy.

"It's a lemon drop," June explained. "Mama gave me two of them. She said I need to save them for a special occasion because candy costs money. I've been holding them for a whole week. I was thinking maybe I could give you one, and I could have one before dinner."

"I think that's a fine idea," Ramona said, reaching into her pocket and finding a couple of pennies. "I'm honored that you would share with me. I'll tell you something. I've been saving something, too."

She held one of the pennies between her thumb and index finger as she squatted down to face the child. Abe Lincoln's chipped nose pointed at June.

"I've been saving my money to do something really special," Ramona said importantly, trying to make a big deal of the penny. "I will give you this penny so you can buy a piece of candy for your mom, and if you eat all of your dinner, I'll give you another penny so you can buy another piece for yourself, too."

The little girl inhaled a gasp as her eyes became large with excitement. She tenderly grabbed the penny, smiled to reveal her bottom two baby teeth were missing, and put the coin in her pocket.

It wasn't long before Leigh-Ann was calling them in for supper. The four crowded around the kitchen table to enjoy chicken-fried steak with black-eyed peas, okra, and a nice hot plate of cornbread. A beautiful pecan pie was cooling on the counter for dessert.

Leigh-Ann Jenkins took pride in educating herself on the news of the day. Not having much of an audience most of the day for such topics when it was only June around the house, she couldn't control herself when she had company.

"And did you hear about that terrible accident in Illinois," Leigh-Ann asked with wide eyes before forking in another bite of the black-eyed peas. "More than 100 coal miners died. It was just awful."

As she explained more of what she had read, Orville politely smiled. He liked Leigh-Ann just fine, but he didn't have time to keep up with anything that wasn't happening on the farm. He didn't even have an opinion on President Truman. Feeling the need to add something to the conversation, he interjected with the one other thing he knew about.

"Ramona is saving up to go to New York," he said uneasily, hoping his daughter would pick it up from there.

Ramona blushed slightly but was ready to help out her daddy.

"Well, I have a lot more saving to do," Ramona said, placing her fork down as if to signify she had a lot to tell. "All these years I've been dancing and singing here, and Miss Taylor says there is nothing left for her to teach me here."

Ramona and Leigh-Ann took turns igniting topics, while Orville was attentive and did his best to look interested. The conversation carried over as Orville grabbed seconds, and Leigh-Ann encouraged little June to clean her plate. When all were finished, they enjoyed generous portions of the pecan pie, with Orville once again going back for seconds. June sat in her mother's lap as she tried to stay awake long enough to finish her piece of the dessert.

Ramona was in the middle of telling everyone about the latest film with Fred and Ginger when Orville quickly perked his head up as if staring at something on the ceiling that wasn't really there. Without having to utter a word, the three adults became quiet.

A dull hum could be heard outside, and it was quickly getting louder. It was as if a large locomotive was speeding its way through the fields without any tracks.

Orville shot up, knocking his chair backwards.

"Get to the storm shelter," Orville yelled as he ran towards the barn to let the animals out of their stables.

The sky was darker than it should have been. As Ramona stood up, she could see the twister. The two-mile-wide storm was bigger than she could have ever imagined. Leigh-Ann had a panicked look on her face as she was pulled from her chair by Ramona.

They sprinted to the back of the house and raced twenty more yards to the concrete lined shelter, Leigh-Ann holding June tightly to her chest. The child's screams were being drowned out by the fast-moving storm. The apron that was still tied around Leigh-Ann's waist flew off as if snatched by a large, unseen hand.

Ramona arrived at the shelter first. She struggled with the metal door as the hinges were rusty, making it difficult to open and close. She was being pelted by flying debris as pieces of wood, rock, and dirt cut into her skin.

Ramona finally pulled the door open as Leigh-Ann and June arrived on the spot. She pushed them down the steps, and quickly turned to look for her father.

"Daddy!" she screamed, but she could not even hear her own voice as the F5 tornado headed straight for the farm.

Leigh Ann and June huddled in the storm cellar. It was not much bigger than a closet. Four adults would be very snug in there huddled on the floor.

Instinctively, Ramona ran back toward where her father had gone. As she rounded the side of the house, the roof was being ripped off the top of the barn. Frozen in her tracks, the tornado quickly crumbled what was left of the structure, sucked it up into the vortex and it was gone.

More debris pelted Ramona and she was now covered in red mud being spit out by the funnel. The storm had sucked more than a foot of water out of a nearby lake. Again, she screamed, but there was no sound. Just the storm. The sound so deafening, she wouldn't have been surprised to see a freight train fall out of the sky.

Finally coming to her senses, Ramona realized she didn't have time to circle the house back to the shelter. She ran through the open door of the house as the screen door snapped off into oblivion. She jumped into the bathtub, wrapped her arms around the led plumbing, and covered her face, unable to hear her own screams. There was a loud crack and a scene from the Wizard of Oz briefly flashed in her mind before she passed out.

It was still dark when Ramona came to. The sound of a chicken clucking brought her back. She was still in the bathtub, wrapped around the plumbing. She was covered in mud. She opened her eyes to see the chicken next to the tub. Most of its feathers were missing. Replaying what had happened in her mind seemed to have taken hours, but it really was only seconds. Nothing made sense. She shouldn't have seen the sky overhead, but she did. Half of the house was gone. Part of the side bedroom and all but two interior walls around the bathroom and the bathtub were there. Nothing more. The twister hit the house with a glancing blow, but it was enough.

Ramona rose slowly, still not able to take in the full devastation that was before her because of the darkness. Looking over her shoulder, she saw that the barn was indeed gone. No sign of Orville. Perhaps in shock, Ramona couldn't cry. No tears would come.

Trees were splintered and uprooted. The woods that led out of the farm now had a tunnel carved through them as if leading something large into town. Where trees remained, large objects that didn't belong could be seen caught in the branches.

Out of habit, Ramona walked out of the house in the spot where the front door used to be, except there was not even a wall there. Nothing. She turned and walked to the back of the house, picking up speed as she found the entrance to the shelter. The metal door had been ripped off its rusted hinges. Leigh-Ann and June were not inside either.

Broadway seemed farther away.

MAY 1949

MULVANE, KANSAS

The movement is what caught his eye and snapped Buster out of his blank stare at nothing for the last ten minutes. Buster had seen the boy earlier on his way to the shop. With the window of his weather-beaten pickup truck down, he saw the young black boy in the dirty clothes walking on the railroad tracks as he drove past the Sante Fe Depot, eventually pulling into the barber shop.

It could be his shop soon if he wanted it. Now thirty years old, Buster, whose real name was William, had trouble figuring out what his next move would be since coming back from the war five years ago. He made it back without a scratch or scar. At least none that could be seen on the outside. The nightmares continued. The blackouts still happened too. He didn't know why he would get so angry sometimes. Working at dad's barbershop wasn't what he had planned on for a career. In fact, he really didn't know what to do, but having somewhere to go everyday gave him a sense of purpose. It kept him calm, too, at least while he was there.

As Buster sat on the bench in front of the shop sipping his black coffee, he saw the boy walking up the sidewalk, looking up toward the sky. White puffy clouds and blue sky. It looked like it would be a nice day in the small town of about a thousand folks. Another sip of coffee, and Buster went inside.

Dad didn't come in on Thursdays, so it was just Buster and J.P. working the chairs today. J.P. was fifty, a little younger than Buster's dad, but he looked older. Mostly bald up top with a bad comb-over. He was only about five and a half feet tall and thirty pounds overweight. A stark contrast to Buster. Still handsome on the outside with dark hair combed neatly to the side, fit and clean shaven. Buster never had much to talk about with J.P., so he wasn't really a fan of Thursdays. That's why he spent a lot of time outside on the bench when he wasn't cutting hair. Getting lost in his thoughts was getting more common.

J.P. was busy with a customer. Not that Alfred's thin gray mane took much time to trim, but the two would sit and argue over everything under the sun for at least an hour. This happened a couple of times per week as Alfred was one of the few that would actually come in for a straight razor shave. He was there for the warm towel and conversation. "The experience" is what he called it.

Buster sat in the barber's chair opposite Alfred but did not speak. He quickly lost track of the conversation, and himself, as his mind drifted elsewhere without his knowing it. He was back on Bougainville in the Solomon Islands for a moment pulling bodies that had piled up in the sand. The sound of the bell on the door as it opened brought him back to Kansas. He was staring at himself in the mirror and didn't know it. He always felt a chill when he came back from his daydream and remembered how scared he had been, wishing he had been braver.

The little boy from down the road had walked in, took one step, and froze. J.P. and Alfred had simultaneously stopped their banter and both heads swiveled in the boy's direction.

Buster leaned in, bringing his head a little closer to the eight-year old's level before the older men could say anything.

There wasn't a "white's only" sign in the shop, but it had pretty much been implied per custom. Like many parts of Kansas, Mulvane wasn't immune to the prejudices of the day, but Buster thought it was getting better. Ku Klux Klan membership had somewhat peaked in the 1920s, but William Allen White's name was still very polarizing in some parts after his failed run to become governor on an anti-KKK platform back in '24.

"Hey fella," Buster said. "What can I do for you?"

The boy opened his mouth once or twice, but no words came out at first. He looked back at the door as if realizing he had made a mistake and wanted to leave, but his feet wouldn't cooperate.

"Aren't you Leonard Thompson's boy?" Buster asked, already knowing the answer.

Leonard Thompson fought in the war, too, but he didn't make it back. He was in the Navy. His ship, the *USS Long*, was sunk after a Kamikaze attack in 1945.

"I was thirsty," the boy started.

"This ain't no café, boy," Alfred said, raising his voice.

Buster hopped out of the chair, landing between the older men and the boy, thus interrupting Alfred.

"Well, you're too young for coffee," Buster said. "How about a glass of water?"

The boy nodded.

"Now see here," J.P. said. "What do you think your daddy will say ..."

"I don't know, but it's my business to tell him," Buster interrupted as he dumped his coffee in the sink and began filling the mug with cool water.

"Thank you," the boy said, almost at a whisper. "My mama said we was going to see my grandpappy and grandma on Saturday. I been saving my money from shining shoes at the station. So, I was thinking I could do something to look nice and was wondering ..."

"Brave kid," Buster thought as he scooped up the child before he could finish and placed him in his chair.

Alfred and J.P. stood with mouths agape, now focusing on Buster instead of the little boy. Neither could get an intelligible word out as they looked at each other in protest.

Buster spun the chair away from the men, then stood behind the boy facing them. Buster's usually handsome demeanor instantly changed. His hair was suddenly out of place dangling down his forehead. He held the straight razor at mid-chest; not exactly threatening, but disturbing nonetheless to the older men, who now chose to be silent.

Buster walked back in front of the chair, reflexively put his hair back in place, and fiddled with the radio until he found music to his liking. He placed an apron around the boy's neck as he sipped his water. Buster picked up his sheers, snapping them open and closed in quick succession. Buster had never cut a black person's hair. The boy's afro just needed some trimming up to make it all look even.

"How hard could it be?" Buster thought to himself, his smile returning.

Buster made small talk while the boy sipped his water, doing his best to keep his head still. J.P. and Alfred still weren't happy. They were talking in low voices, for once not arguing with each other as they now had a common enemy for the moment. The boy talked about his grandparents but didn't mention his father at first. It soon worked its way into the conversation.

"You fought in the war, didn't you, Sir?" the boy asked.

"I did," Buster said. "Just like your daddy."

The boy seemed surprised that Buster knew. He was more at ease now.

There really wasn't much hair to cut, but Buster gave him the full treatment. For once, he was able to concentrate without drifting. He trimmed the hair where it needed to be trimmed. He washed his head in the sink, which drew a guffaw from J.P. He even wrapped the boy's face in a warm towel, even though there wasn't a shave before it. This was a silent dig at Alfred, as the little black boy was now getting "the experience."

When he was done, Buster loosened the apron and gently brushed some talcum powder around the boy's neck. The little boy smiled because it smelled good. Buster then grabbed his little mirror so the boy could see how he looked. He even nodded in approval without realizing it.

"I never asked you your name," Buster said as the boy hopped out of the chair.

"It's Leonard, Jr., Sir," the boy said, looking at Buster in the eye for the first time. "My mama just calls me 'Junior.'"

Leonard began fishing at the coins in his pocket, while J.P. propped up a badly framed pricelist and put it on the chair so that the boy would surely be able to see it. It should have cost at least fifty cents.

Buster flipped the menu face down with his comb and squatted before the boy. Leonard held out his hand, holding a few nickels and a penny. The nickels were all face down, while the penny with the chip in Lincoln's nose lay face up.

"This should take care of it," Buster said as he picked up only the wounded penny. "You come back any time, you hear?"

Leonard nodded, smiled and was out the door with this fresh haircut, a clean face, and something he hadn't come in with, dignity.

Alfred made a show of leaving, aggressively thumping his newspaper under his arm. He flung the door open, shaking his head in disbelief.

"Nice going," J.P. said sarcastically. "You probably lost me one of my best customers for a while."

Buster smiled a little bit. For once he felt brave. Now he and J.P. finally had something to talk about.

NEAR UNSAN, NORTH KOREA

When the first bullet smashed through Jacob's rib cage, it knocked him backwards as it exited through his back. The second and third shots knocked him down. At first, he thought he had been hit by a baseball bat, as the wind was knocked from his lungs.

The constant hail of rifle and machine gun fire made different sounds than Jacob thought they would. As he lay in the mud, he momentarily forgot that he was bleeding badly from his side and legs. The smoke from the forest fires, intentionally set by the enemy to keep the U.N. forces from gaining accurate aerial reconnaissance, continued to blanket the valley as it had for several days.

A bullet hitting the wet dirt sometimes made a dull sound. A bullet striking a helmet made an awful "thang" sound. A bullet hitting flesh reminded him of the click of a camera. Somehow, that sound was always louder than the rat-tat-tat of machine gun fire and the pop of a rifle shot. At least that's what he thought when the first bullet hit him, and he found himself staring up at the smoky sky.

The sounds of the gunfire were interrupted by screaming. Then Jacob realized it was he who was screaming. When he was first hit, it didn't hurt as much as he thought it would. Then it really burned. He could feel the pressure of the blood leaking inside his body.

He twisted his head to the right. Lying next to him was Francis. Everyone called Francis "The Governor." He wasn't really a politician, but he had talked about how was going to run for town council when he got home to Indiana. Nobody would be calling him anything anymore, and "The Governor" would be going home in casket, if he was lucky. His dead brown eyes stared back at Jacob. His mouth gaped open with a look of anguish as if waiting to exhale. His teeth were covered with his own dark blood.

In a blur, a soldier slid on his knees between them. Thankfully, an American soldier. It was that priest that everyone spoke about. Jacob was Jewish and didn't know the priest well, but he knew stories. Stories of how he would say Mass, using a jeep as an altar. He would hear confessions every day for soldiers, even if they weren't Catholic. There were no atheists in battle.

Jacob couldn't recall his name, but he watched as the priest quickly performed last rights on "The Governor." No bullet seemed to come close to him.

The priest turned his glance to Jacob. "Can you move, son?"

Jacob realized he had stopped screaming. His wounds were agonizing, but he felt a momentary sense of peace as he nodded his head. The priest helped him stand on one leg and began to drag him back further away from the storm of bullets. It was then he noticed the valley was littered with bodies from the 8th Calvary, some were still moving. Many were still. The ones that were still firing were trying to make themselves small out there in the open, huddling behind any barrier or foxhole they could find.

A pair of GIs in a ditch, twenty feet away, were mowing down waves of Chinese with a Browning .50 caliber machine gun they had taken off a now flaming truck. Dozens of Chinese were falling down as the Browning sprayed indiscriminately, but where those soldiers fell there were seemingly hundreds more Chinese filling their place. Chinese that weren't supposed to have entered the war. At least, that's what the generals had told them.

Falling into a shallow foxhole surrounded by a few sandbags, Jacob cried out, but his voice was drowned out by bazooka fire from a GI in the foxhole a few yards away.

There were blasts from bugles and terrible screams as the Chinese soldiers continued their overwhelming advance. Mortars rained down from all directions. Dirt, rocks, and the occasional body part would fall back to earth a second later.

Jacob grabbed the priest's arm as the holy man bent over him. He realized then that a medic was already attending to him, and he felt the priest's fingers on his forehead.

"I'm giving you the last rights," the priest said. "Not all of us are going to make it home."

The priest did so in English instead of Latin. Jacob thought he was going to pass out. Loss of blood or sheer panic would equally be culpable. The priest finished his prayer and gently grabbed Jacob's chin to get his attention. He noticed the priest was clean-shaven. Everyone else had five days of stubble, but the priest's face was dirty, yet smooth. As Jacob locked eyes with the priest, he wanted to speak, and all the sounds of war seemed suddenly quiet.

"Do you see this?" the priest said as he pulled a penny out of his front pocket. "Sergeant Murphy gave me this. He said it was lucky. Maybe it is. Hold it for me until I get back. Whatever prayers you know, say them now. God be with you, my son."

Sergeant Murphy wasn't really all that lucky. In fact, Sergeant Murphy was already dead. Murphy had told the priest that his little brother gave the penny to him after he was drafted as a good luck charm. He told the priest to mail it back to his brother in Pembroke Pines, Florida, after the war, and to tell him that he thought of him every day. The priest didn't mention this part of the story to Jacob.

Dumbfounded, Jacob was able to hold the coin in his blood-soaked fingers. Abraham Lincoln looked wounded too with blood covering his chipped nose. "In God We Trust" arched across the top of the penny, and Jacob had a moment of lucidity. The morphine syrette the medic had given him was already dulling his pain to the point that he thought he might live after all.

Like an echo, Jacob heard the priest's last words to him again, "God be with you, my son."

Jacob tucked the penny in his front jacket pocket and used what strength he had left to peek over the sandbags. The priest was already fifty yards away, dragging another wounded man to a foxhole. Scanning east, he saw another GI among a pile of bodies. He was lobbing hand grenades at the advancing enemy. Then he lay still, as if he were dead, only to resume his personal bombardment moments later. His rifle had no ammunition, and this game of possum was his only defense. When he ran out of hand grenades, he pulled the body of a dead soldier over him to hide. The dead man's once olive drab uniform was mostly a wet dark purple now.

A jet buzzed low overhead, dropping napalm on advancing Chinese, perhaps only 200 yards away. Hundreds were incinerated. More were coming.

Craning his head back and forth, he caught site of the priest again. Unarmed, he was hopping through the battlefield as the Chinese became visible from nearly every direction. He was like a ghost. Not a single bullet had his name on it.

A corporal with a field telephone was now in the foxhole along with Lieutenant Danby. Danby had one finger in his ear and was screaming into the telephone. The panic in

Danby's voice told Jacob all he needed to know. They were nearly surrounded, and greatly outnumbered. Surrender was not an option. Jacob didn't know the difference between North Koreans and the Chinese, but the communists did not have reputations for taking prisoners or treating them well if they did.

"We're going to get you on a jeep and get you out of here," the medic said.

He didn't hear the mortar shell exploding into the nearest jeep that was parked less than one hundred feet away, but he saw the vehicle instantly burst into flames.

"But not that one," Jacob thought, almost laughing as he reflexively pointed at the vehicle.

Jacob was close to passing out again. He tried to take another look over the sandbag. No priest this time. Just screams, smoke and more soldiers falling to the ground.

Lieutenant Danby was now laying on his stomach next to Jacob, firing into the enemy with the corporal's rifle. Corporal Jernigan didn't need it anymore. A bullet had exploded his cheekbone, taking much of his face away. The medic was nowhere to be seen.

"Shit! Shit! Shit!" Danby shouted as the last of his bullets left the barrel.

"In God we trust," Jacob whispered. It was the only prayer he could think of as he began to black out.

CORVALLIS, OREGON

"Just one more day," Marie told herself as she lay in bed, staring at the ceiling. "Give me one more day."

Getting up for work was getting tougher. She sat up in bed and eyed the various prescription pill bottles on the nightstand, wondering if they were really worth taking or if she was already too far gone.

Maria sat up and took a deep breath. She admired the photo of her husband, Dennis, and her young son, T.J., on the dresser. They were her rock.

"Just one more day," Maria said to herself again.

She put on her brave face in the shower, and willed her pain to run down the drain, temporarily.

Delicately eating a piece of buttered toast as she walked to the car, she was embarrassed when Glen caught her in midbite.

"Good morning, Marie," her neighbor called out as he walked to his car on the way to work at the same time.

Marie offered her first smile of the day, started the engine, and made the twenty-five-minute drive to work. "The Farm," as she called it, was an orphanage. She always loved being around children. Their joy and laughter could make her deepest pain subside, at least for a little while. Marie did her best to teach them some life skills, hoping each day that some of the children would be gone because they had been adopted.

Mostly she loved holding them. She was always met with an embrace and a smile, and she would give them the same in return. She loved reading to them and having them read to her. She wanted to give them hope each day, and in some ways, they gave her hope and strength to get through one more day.

She also taught the children some basic English, history, and math as best she could. The Farm didn't have many books, but she would make do. Last week, she gave a lesson on the Civil War and passed around a penny so the children could get an idea of what Abraham Lincoln looked like in lieu of no textbooks.

Benjamin was her favorite. He was twelve and often lamented that he would never be adopted because he was too old. He was a skinny, gangly child, who despite getting somewhat decent meals at The Farm, still looked as if he had a lot of catching up to do from a nutritional standpoint. His skin was pale, and sometimes he shook. He had undiagnosed ticks with his face, and some would-be parents seemed turned off by any child who was less than perfect. Marie would never admit he was a homely child because she loved him, and he loved her.

After the Civil War lesson, she gave the penny to Benjamin as a reward for answering a couple of questions correctly. She frowned at her inability to smooth out the scratch on the president's face, but Benjamin was happy just the same. He would often hold it up to her to show that he still had the coin and how much he treasured it.

While she wished for him to have a family, she felt guilty about being sad if she wasn't able to spend time with him. Although he knew nothing of her pain, sometimes he was her reminder that she too would be missed if she lost her fight to hang on. His warm embrace when she left each day made her feel like she had made a difference, at least for that day.

She would never look back as she went to her car at the end of the day, but there was always something that happened each day that made her look forward to coming back tomorrow. Just one more day.

Marie drove home in silence. The smile and joy slowly slipping away with each passing mile.

As Marie entered her house, she dropped her purse on the floor of the living room, and collapsed on the couch, physically and mentally exhausted.

She didn't have the energy to make dinner and wondered if there was even a TV dinner left in the icebox. She glanced at the decanter of bourbon on top of the liquor cabinet.

"That's how this all started," she said with a frown and not for the first time.

Methodically, Marie stood and walked to the family photo on the mantel, discarding the dust on top of the frame with her index finger.

She whispered, "Just one more day."

Marie followed her nightly routine and walked to the nightstand. Opening one of her prescription bottles, she poured the contents into her hand. There must have been two dozen of the little white pills. One pill would help ease her pain. It would help her find a hazy sleep.

A dozen pills would likely take all her pain away for good. She thought about that every night. Every night for the last eight months. She wanted it to end, but she always thought about the children at The Farm who needed her.

The same questions always ran through her head. "They would be sad, wouldn't they? Would they come to her funeral? Did they even know I was sick?"

Marie had promised herself that the day she didn't make a difference, was the day she would give in.

She had made a difference today.

Again.

Like she always did.

"Just one more day," she said softly while squeezing the pills in her palm.

Her eyes found the photo of Dennis and T.J., like they always did. She could hear his voice on the phone, "We're having a great time on the trip, but we miss you! Don't worry though, we'll be home tomorrow. Just one more day."

The truck driver that sideswiped them had been drinking. The car had been so mangled and twisted in the accident that Marie couldn't bring herself to identify the bodies. Glen had done that for her.

She thought about getting T.J.'s clothes out of his closet to bring to Ben, but she still couldn't bring herself to enter his room. The bed had been made for eight months; his toys collecting dust.

Pouring all but one of the pills back into the bottle, Marie took her dosage. She would let the medicine help her sleep and try to make it through one more time.

"Give me one more day with them," Marie cried, knowing her appeal would not be realized. "Just one more day."

SAN ANTONIO, TEXAS

"Swing and a miss, strike three," Gene Redd announced with a touch of disappointment.

As the game dragged on to the eighth inning, Gene was still trying to make it interesting. The longtime minor league radio broadcaster couldn't wait for this game to be over. With his San Antonio Missions trailing by nine runs this late in the game on a humid Texas night, Gene was looking forward to getting out of the ballpark and wrapping his hands around a cold beer.

He disgustedly scratched another "K" in his scorebook with his stubby pencil after Dyck had struck out for the third time a moment ago.

Gene took pride in being a professional in all his broadcasts over the years, but it had been a long season, and long night in particular. Now forty-two years old, Gene was still chasing the same dream as all those young ball players on the field, although it was less likely he was going to be moving up to a Major League team at this point in his career.

These were the days that he lamented some of his life choices and not settling down with a wife and having children, while constantly watching a child's game played by grown men in the hopes that he would be doing this for the Yankees or the Dodgers someday. He still loved it, but there were many days when he thought he would gladly trade it all for having a catch with a young son and treating him to an ice cream after a game. If only he had switched his priorities and chased that dream long ago.

But that was not to be.

Still, he coaxed some enthusiasm into his voice for the benefit of anyone that was listening.

"One out in the eighth, and it looks like Coach Fox will send up a pinch-hitter for McCloskey," Gene reported as he tried to read the number of the player coming out of the dugout. Because he didn't recognize the face or shape of the body, he assumed it must be the new kid. The announcement by the P.A. announcer confirmed his suspicion and he continued.

"Making his professional baseball debut will be the youngster, Harold….." Gene fumbled with his notes as the new kid was not on any roster yet, and he only had the info that Coach Fox gave him before the game. Finding his note card, he carried on. "Harold Von Hindenburk."

Gene didn't trust his own handwriting and covered his microphone with one hand, while delivering a loud whisper to Dave, the P.A. announcer, at the other end of the press box. "Is that how you say it?"

"Vandenberg. Van-den-berg," came the reply.

Gene nodded and played it off as if he had said it correctly all along.

"So, here's Harold Vandenberg. He was just signed to the club earlier this week. He's eighteen years old from Fredericksburg."

Gene tried to replay the conversation with Coach Fox from earlier in the day. "He's some kid that we actually plucked off a farm. He was supporting his mama as best he could. No father in the picture apparently. His high school coach and I go back a bit, and he told me about him, so we had someone go out there, and he didn't look too bad."

Closing his eyes, Gene relayed the appropriate parts of the story as young Harold made his way to home plate. He penciled his name on his scoresheet and continued.

"He's a right-handed batter and is slightly crouched at the plate," Gene described. "The first pitch from Cannon is a fastball, and it's up high for ball one to Harold Vandenberg."

Saying the name again awoke something inside of Gene. "How do I know that name?" he thought to himself.

"The young man is said to be able to play shortstop or third base and could also play in the outfield," Gene resumed his reporting. "He's back in the box. Cannon delivers. Swing and a miss on another fastball. The youngster looked over-matched on that one. It's a long way from high school for Mr. Vandenberg."

Again, Gene's senses tingled in saying the name. So, he said it again. "Harold Vandenberg at the plate with a one-one count here in the eighth inning. The Missions trailing it, nine-nothing. It has been a dismal night all around with three errors and only one hit for San Antonio tonight."

Harold adjusted his cap and stepped back in for the next pitch.

"Cannon leans in for the sign. Here's the one-one pitch. Whoa, swing and miss on a big curve ball, and Vandenberg was nowhere close. Welcome to the Texas League, kid. A ball and two strikes now on Harold Vandenberg."

Carl, the newspaper writer, was chatting loudly with Dave in the press box about the origin of the name Vandenberg. "You don't see a lot of them Hebrews in baseball."

"I thought he was German," Dave retorted.

Gene's head immediately whispered "Fahn-din-beerg" and his eyes became like saucers as he nearly missed the call of the next pitch.

"Ball two, high," Gene stammered.

"Fahn-din-beerg," Gene said, not realizing he had said it out loud and then catching himself. "Cannon deals two-two. The rookie just gets a piece of that fastball to stay alive."

Scrambling through his notes again, he saw Fredericksburg. "It couldn't be," he thought to himself. "What was her name? Nah. That can't be right."

Gene immediately went back in time, his neurons firing in a rapid pace. Fredericksburg. A hunting trip. A small restaurant and bar. The bar maid. A face. Elloise? Ella? Elsa? Yes, Elsa.

"Elsa Vandenberg," Gene mouthed silently. "It couldn't be. I mean, that had to be before the war. Maybe '39?" He started doing math with his fingers and squinted down at the young man at the plate.

Then coming back to the present. "Another two-two pitch... it's high and tight and Vandenberg, spins out of the way and crashes to the dirt."

Gene noticed the boy actually smiled as he dusted himself off, and he knew. He knew that smile.

With renewed vigor, Gene settled back into his call. Cupping the microphone with one hand, in an almost loving gesture to the inanimate object that nobody noticed.

"The three-two from Cannon. The fastball is hit high and deep to left field. Nash goes back to the warning track, to the wall... he looks up, and it's gone!"

Gene exploded out of his chair, knocking it over backwards. "Touch 'em all, son!"

Dave and Carl looked perplexed at the sudden vigor by Gene in a game that was all but over.

"Harold Vandenberg has hit a home run in his first at bat, and that brings the score to nine to one," Gene shouted while pumping his arm excitedly. He then readjusted his shirt and pants after nearly coming undressed with his call. "The young man from the farm, well, he just..."

And for the first time in his career, Gene was at a loss for words. He marveled quietly for a moment as Harold rounded the bases and touched home plate. The handful of fans still in attendance applauded politely.

Dave and Carl shrugged.

Gene remained standing as he finished the game. The Missions did not score again and lost 10-1, but Gene didn't care. Each out was described as if it were the most marvelous play to ever happen on the baseball diamond.

He rushed through his postgame remarks and signed off. Grabbing his fedora, Gene glanced at a mirror to smooth his hair. He was about fifteen pounds overweight now, but he thought he looked great. He straightened his tie and made his way to the small dressing room behind the dugout.

Coach Fox greeted him with a surprised look.

"Whoa, Gene, what are you doing in here? I can't grab a beer tonight since we've got that doubleheader tomorrow."

"Never mind that, Foxy," Gene said. "Where's the kid?" Gene was dodging his head side to side, hoping it would help him see around corners.

"I think he already walked out," Fox said, rubbing his stubbly chin. "The Jacksons were kind enough to let him use a spare room for a while since he just got here. He walked out, still in his uniform. He looked really happy to be wearing it. Yeah, so the kid looked OK. Maybe I'll start him tomorrow."

Gene was no longer listening. He sprinted out of the dressing room without saying goodbye and raced toward the exit where a few cars were exiting with a dusty cloud behind each. Looking left and then right, Gene saw a baseball in the dirt beyond the leftfield fence. He picked up the home run ball that nobody wanted and stared at it, wishing it could talk.

"Hey mister," a voice called out. "I wonder if you'd let me have that. I don't really have anything to trade, but I thought I'd show it to my ma."

Gene turned to Harold and smiled greatly. He soft-tossed the dirty baseball over to him, chuckling at his first chance to play catch with his son he never knew, and immediately sad for the lifetime he had missed. Fishing through his pockets, he found a few dimes and an odd penny with a scratch on the front and looked back up. "Hey kid, do you like ice cream?"

STINESVILLE, INDIANA

Sal peeked in the rearview mirror at the old woman sitting in the back of his cab. He had helped Louise climb into his cab from her little home in nearby Ellettsville about thirty minutes ago. She didn't give him a specific destination, but she asked him to take her to Stinesville.

"Don't drive too fast," she had asked peacefully and hadn't spoken since.

At first, he was a little put off as he liked to know exactly where he was going. It was a slow day, however, and Sal didn't expect a lot of fares, so he took his time snaking through the various roads in the '53 two-tone yellow Ford as she quietly stared out the window. On a slow day, this could be a big fare.

Pulling onto Elm Street, Louise spoke again as the memories flooded in.

"My father worked in the quarries all his life," Louise announced. "He cut the limestone."

Sal smiled politely, and although he began to tune her out, he kept nodding his head as she went on for ten minutes about her dad, the quarry, and the limestone. He was more concerned about trying to tune in Bobby Darrin on the radio as "Mac the Knife" crackled in and out.

Louise went on and on about how limestone was in such high demand after the big fires in Boston and Chicago.

"Daddy said there were lots of stone cutters from Europe that came over," Louise said. "At first, he didn't like some of the Italian fellas, but he learned a few things from them and decided they were OK.

"Turn left here," she said suddenly.

Fortunately, Sal was still driving slowly and made the turn.

"This is where we lived," Louise had a little excitement and disappointment in her voice simultaneously as they pulled up to a white house with mostly chipped paint. The house had not been lived in for years and was in disrepair.

"We ate a lot of our dinners right there on the front porch," Louise beamed. "And see that window on the side? That's where Dottie and I slept. We had a cocker spaniel, we called her 'Daisy.' She slept in there with us."

"Is this where you'd like to get out ma'am?" Sal asked.

"Oh, no," Louise said as she proceeded to share her memories of the little house. "And see that little house across the way? That's where Don and I lived when we were married. He worked the quarries, too. My two boys were born there. Oh, I must take them back here when they come back to visit."

Sal smiled politely, wondering if the fare was going to take more time than it was worth.

"Let's keep going," Louise said as she pointed back down the road.

Sal was fiddling with the radio as they drove over the bridge that crossed Jack's Defeat Creek when Louise spoke up again. "Stop here," she said.

Sal was a little surprised about her wanting to stop, but seeing there were no other cars behind them, he obliged. Louise had a happy look on her face, like a coy child who was about to reveal a big secret.

"I kissed a boy for the first time right down there," Louise beamed with a little chuckle. "I was seven. Brian was his name. His daddy was a stone carver and had come over from Scotland. We were catching frogs with Dottie. I just thought he was the cutest thing with that bright orange hair of his."

Louise may have been sitting in the back of the cab, but at that moment, she was a little girl back in 1883.

"He caught a big one, and he let me hold it without my even asking," Louise relived. "So, I just gave him a quick peck right on the mouth; Brian, that is. Not the frog, you understand. Boy, was he surprised!"

Sal faked a smile.

"We spent a lot of time down there," she continued. "We used to swim in the shallows. Oh, and when the trains went by, we had to hold our ears. When I got older, my boys used to swim there, too. I need to take them back here next time they visit."

Louise got quiet for a moment. She was lost in her childhood.

"OK, let's go," Louise said as she returned to the present.

Sal looked at his watch. This was taking too long for his liking, but at least the meter was running. He pushed his gray cap further up on his forehead, pursed his lips, and the cab once again jerked forward as he put it into gear.

Louise never told him where they were going but would just tell him when to turn and when to slow down. As they drove by where the old mill used to be, she told the story of how it had burned down, and the town began to die.

"We had to leave so Don could find work," Louise said as she stared at the ghosts outside her window. "I hated to leave. This was the only place I knew. I guess I was about thirty at the time."

Her spirits picked up and faded once again as they drove down Main Street. Naturally, all the old store fronts were made of limestone. Sadly, many of them were closed.

"Stop here," Louise asked as they pulled in front of the Mercantile building. She opened her purse and pulled out a few coins. Leaning forward, she placed one hand on Sal's shoulder and held the other hand up high, signaling for him to accept the coins. "Will you go in and get us a cold pop?"

Sal took the coins and thumbed the four dimes and five old pennies. The pennies were sticky, as if a hard candy had melted on them. He tried to scratch the residue off Abe Lincoln's chipped nose. Sal used his shoulder to open the driver's side door and walked up to the front door of the two-story building. The knob didn't budge. Looking through the dirty windows, he couldn't tell if it was just closed because it was Sunday or if it had been closed for a while. Either way, he wasn't getting an RC cola.

"Sorry, ma'am," Sal said as he flopped back into the driver's seat. "Looks like they're closed."

He reached over the passenger seat beside him where he had a mason jar filled with water. He held it up to offer it to the old woman, but Louise smiled and waved him off. Sal turned to return her coins, but she was looking at the windows and was back in time again.

"Me and my boys were sitting right there on those steps the first time we saw an automobile come through downtown," Louise declared. "I'll have to remind them about that when they come visit."

By now, Sal knew not to ask, so he just waited for it. He knew that this was how his day was going to be spent. There was no sense in fighting it. Eyeing the meter to make sure it was still running, he pressed on.

As Louise came back to the present she continued to serve as a tour guide, recalling memories of her father and her two sons. Sal didn't ask any questions, but he started to take an interest as he warmed up to the old woman. He had ridden through the old town before, but never really spent time in it. There was a certain joy and hidden sadness as she rediscovered something around every turn.

"I wish my boys could see this," Louise repeated many times along the way.

Heading east on Walker Lane, Sal glanced back. Louise was looking tired, but suddenly her eyes got bigger, so he reflexively slowed down in anticipation of another stop.

"It's not here," Louise said, disappointedly. She looked back and forth a little nervously.

"What is it," Sal said, engaging her for the first time.

"The old schoolhouse," Louise said. "It was around here somewhere. It was just one room. It got so cold in the winter back then. We all huddled together in the classroom to keep warm while we learned our lessons. I remember not wanting to get out of bed sometimes. Daddy would heat up big rocks and put them in our beds to keep us warm at night."

She signaled it was alright to continue, and Sal carefully put the cab into gear so there was minimal lurch this time. A few minutes later Louise spoke up again and asked for another stop.

"I'd like to get out," Louise said.

Sal quickly jumped out and walked around to the back to open the rear door. He held out his hand to help Louise. She accepted, thanked him, and slowly shuffled on to the grass.

Looking left and right, Sal didn't see anything of significance. No buildings. Not even abandoned homes. Just grass and trees with green leaves. He pushed his cap further up on his forehead again.

Louise was already about fifteen feet ahead of him. The old woman moved better than he thought. She didn't invite him to follow, but he did anyway. It was the first time she had stepped out of the cab all day, so there must be something worth seeing.

She bowed beneath some tree branches and stepped through tall grass before the woods opened into a small field. A series of headstones rose up from the ground; the whitish-gray limestones stood out among all the green.

He didn't know if she was aware of his presence, so Sal stayed ten feet behind her. She was whispering. He couldn't tell if she was praying or having a conversation, but for the first time today, Louise clearly was not talking to Sal. This was more private.

The quiet conversation went on for fifteen minutes. Sal didn't move from his spot. Louise was quiet for a moment, then she took a deep breath and relaxed her shoulders as she exhaled. Was it contentment? Was it defeat? Sal wasn't sure.

Louise turned and was slightly startled and amused to see Sal standing there with a quizzical look on his face. She smiled as she passed him.

He let her get a few yards ahead of him before walking briskly to examine the head stones. The names and dates were pretty weathered with the lack of attention over the years, but he saw what he needed to see. Turning back to see Louise, he nodded at the headstones before jogging to get in step with the old woman.

Holding the door open for her, Sal again took her hand to help the little woman get into the seat.

"I'm ready to go back home now," Louise said, staring at nothing.

Sal tipped his cap, took his place behind the wheel, and gently got the cab moving forward again. "If you'd like to go back next weekend to look for that schoolhouse, I'd be glad to take you," he said, knowing that her sons would never be making the trip with her. They were already here.

Only a few minutes into the drive, Sal looked into his rear-view mirror and was prepared to ask if she wanted him to stop in town when they got to Ellettsville so she could get something to eat. They had been gone four hours. He didn't need to ask, however. Louise was asleep.

It had been a big day for Louise, living her eighty-three years again in one day.

Sal turned off the meter.

COLUMBIA, MISSOURI

Andrew's tuxedo shirt was already a little tight around the neck. It was ninety degrees and humid, adding to his misery. His wedding day was supposed to be the best day of his life. That's what the twenty-eight-year-old had always been told by his mother, and his soon-to-be bride, Melissa, surely felt that way.

Andrew made the mistake of staying out too late last night for his bachelor party. He was cursing himself for not insisting they do it a night earlier, but then again, not all of the "apostles" would have been back in town by then.

Andrew, Jimmy, Buck, and the Largent twins, Phil, and Matt, were inseparable from middle school through twelfth grade. A teacher once dubbed the group 'The Apostles,' as Buck's full name was Bartholomew, but nobody called him that except his mother. It all changed after they graduated from high school 10 years ago.

Buck had an opportunity to play professional baseball, but a knee injury washed him out of the game after just two years in the minor leagues. He found a job loading bags at Lambert Airport in St. Louis and had been there ever since. His sandy hair was still cropped very short, and hauling suitcases did nothing to hurt his lean, muscular physique.

Phil and Matt went to Mizzou and studied journalism. As fraternal twins, the two couldn't look any less like brothers. Phil was tall and skinny with dark hair. Matt was stout, more vertically challenged, and his brown hair was already receding halfway to the back of his head. Some of the other kids in middle school used to call them "Abbott and Costello," unless Buck was in the room. He wouldn't allow anyone to pick on his friends.

Phil was working as a reporter at a nearby television station, mostly as a writer. The less handsome Matt was a beat writer for the newspaper in Evansville, Indiana. "A face made for a typewriter," he used to say.

Jimmy got out of the Midwest. The guy with all the answers somehow finagled his way into a scholarship at Fordham University in the Bronx, New York. He met all the right people, and later went to law school. Two years later, he's all the way across the country in Los Angeles, and has made a name for himself handling divorce cases, which apparently isn't taboo there.

Jimmy always liked to be a big deal. He felt the need to always be "on." Everything was a game and needed to have some element of fun. His good professional fortune backed up his desired lifestyle.

Andrew stayed in Columbia. Not long after graduation, his father made a call to set up an interview with a friend who sold insurance, and that's where Andrew landed.

Ten years after they all left high school, Andrew's wedding was the first time that all five were together again.

There was no air conditioning in the Catholic church, and Andrew wanted to drink more water, but he was afraid he'd have to pee in the middle of the ceremony. He was well aware that a full-on Catholic wedding was not a short affair. At least an hour, or maybe longer if Father Michael got a little long-winded in his sermon.

Last night started off innocently enough. The 3.2 beer served in Missouri allowed the men to imbibe more than they would have almost anywhere else. Liquor was still hard to come by in Columbia, but Jimmy had smuggled in some tequila and some high-priced vodka. All those drinks didn't mix well, and Andrew vaguely remembered throwing up in his front yard before finally going to bed. His stomach wouldn't allow him to eat any breakfast either.

Now a few minutes before 2 p.m., it had been almost twenty hours since Andrew had eaten anything. Waves of nausea came and went. His head hurt, and he was uncomfortably warm.

"It's time," Buck said as he joined his friends in the little room outside the front of the church.

The five men wore matching tuxedos. White jacket. Black pants.

Andrew stomached one more sip of water from the fountain, wiped his mouth with his hand and put on a brave face. He gave one last look as a single man to his childhood friends and was flooded with memories. He still saw the teenager in all of them. The fun they had. The mistakes they made, and the things nobody knew about.

"Think he'll make it?" Phil said with a smile as they filed out.

Jimmy shook his head and chuckled.

Buck gave him a sour look. Always the responsible one, he was feeling fine after only having two beers and driving the apostles around for much of the evening.

Andrew's stomach gurgled as Melissa walked up toward the altar. Fortunately, the music from the organ drowned out everything. She was beautiful in her white dress. It looked like she had a good night's sleep.

Melissa's dark hair was placed in an intricate bun on the top of her head. Andrew always liked her hair down and how it complimented the round shape of her face, but she was still beautiful. For just a little while, he forgot how miserable he was feeling.

The humidity in the church was unbearable. Andrew repeatedly dabbed his forehead with his handkerchief.

Andrew's face was growing paler as the service went on. From the front pew, Jimmy elbowed Matt, and spoke through the corner of his mouth, "He's not going to make it."

Tilting his head upward, the shortest of the apostles covered his mouth and whispered, "It's fifty-fifty right now."

The cantor was singing the responsorial Psalm in Latin in between the two readings, giving Jimmy another opportunity.

"Five bucks says he doesn't make it," Jimmy said.

"You're on," Matt whispered and gave a thumbs-up.

"I'm in, too," Philip said. "He'll make it."

Buck clenched his teeth and said nothing. He wasn't amused.

Andrew made it through the Gospel reading. Father Michael began his sermon by reading a line from the Gospel of Mark.

"What therefore God hath joined together, let no man put asunder," the priest said as he looked over the congregation.

Jimmy leaned down to Matt and quipped, "I make a living off 'asunder.'"

Matt bit his tongue hard trying not to laugh. Philip did the same and his chest was shaking a little as he tried to subdue his own guffaw. Even Buck was caught off guard, blowing a small snot bubble from his nose as he broke character with an equally amusing schoolgirl giggle.

Andrew wasn't listening to the sermon. He wasn't thinking about his nausea right now, only because he had a sudden strong urge to break wind. Actually, he wasn't sure if it was just gas or if he needed to go to the toilet. Either way, he had to hold it in.

He earned a little bit of a reprieve as Father Michael's sermon was predictable and mercifully, relatively short.

As they stood to exchange vows, Andrew was really sweating. Melissa noticed his discomfort for the first time and gave him a concerned look. Andrew tried to return a look of reassurance as he clenched the cheeks from his rear end. This would be the worst time to let one go. Nowhere to hide.

As the couple exchanged their rings, a short burst of gas silently escaped Andrew. Father Michael didn't hear it. Melissa did. She had a worried look as she saw another bead of sweat roll down Andrew's nose.

"Did he just," Matt whispered through the side of his mouth.

"Mmm-hmmm," Jimmy confirmed without moving his lips so he wouldn't burst out laughing.

It's always funnier in church.

Andrew was now nearly the same shade as his jacket.

"Should we go get him?" Phil asked with legitimate concern.

Game on. Jimmy slyly pulled a coin from his pants pocket, and returning his hands to his side, he made his play. "Heads, no. Tails, OK."

Since everyone else's eyes were on the bride and the groom, only the altar boy noticed when Jimmy simply dropped the penny down his leg and onto the floor. It rolled off his shoe and came to rest on the red carpet. Abe Lincoln's chipped face stared up at the ornately painted ceiling.

Jimmy smiled with satisfaction while the rest of the apostles were secretly saying prayers that their friend would be OK.

Andrew's knees buckled slightly once, and Buck flinched as if ready to hold his friend up before he hit the deck. Father Michael didn't have a clue.

Andrew was thankful to kneel a few minutes later as they prepared to receive communion. When offered the sacramental wine, he put the cup to his lips but didn't actually drink it. He wasn't sure, but he thought he could smell the alcohol in his sweat. He kept trying to think of something else to keep his mind off his urge to throw up. At this point he didn't care about remembering details of his wedding. The nightmare of simultaneously throwing up, passing out, and perhaps even having an accident right there entered his mind more than once.

As the mass ended, Andrew's sweaty hand held that of his new bride. With each step down the aisle, a little more gas escaped. Sometimes silently. Sometimes not. For the first time, Father Michael's olfactory senses were aware that something was "off" as he followed the couple down to the back of the church.

Andrew picked up the pace as they were pelted with rice outside the church. Melissa didn't hear the "putt-putt" with every step as the rice stuck in her hair. Andrew opened the door to the car for his bride, and nervously walked around the back to get into the driver's seat. Melissa waved to the crowd.

As Andrew started the engine, Ray Charles sang "Hit the Road, Jack" after Jimmy had turned the radio up full blast when parking the car there before the ceremony. One last prank. One last game.

As the black 1955 Dodge pulled away from the church, the trail of dented Budweiser cans that were tied to the rear bumper rattled on the hot asphalt.

The empty bottle of tequila Jimmy slipped in Andrew's suitcase wouldn't be found until the morning.

BETHANY, WEST VIRGINIA

The snowball was packed hard and stung as it exploded on Kyle's face just below his left eye. The unwritten rules of the neighborhood were that you couldn't use ice balls in snowball fights.

These guys didn't play by the rules, and the attack wasn't unexpected. At least for Kyle.

Still, it stung, and he felt like crying. Kyle tried to be tough, but he was a beaten man. Well, a beaten eight-year-old. Instinctively he tried to run. It wasn't easy to run in green waterproof snow boots, snow pants, and his heavy winter coat. Plus, he had his sack lunch in one hand and his books strapped together in the other. His stuffy nose sent a trail of watery snot above his lip. He was in no-man's land. Halfway between the walk from his house to his school. No fast way to a safe haven. He knew it was coming, but he always hoped it wouldn't.

"Maybe today will be different," Kyle would say to himself every morning when he left the security of his house to walk to school. He used to cry about it when he was in his bed alone at night. Not anymore. He day-dreamed about being able to stand up to the bullies and to fire back. He saw himself as a superhero, kicking and punching his assailants until they begged for mercy.

But that was only in his dreams.

The lead bully, Brian, and his crony, Pauley, continued to pelt him with hard-packed snowballs. With each blow, Kyle expected to see small pebbles packed in for extra pain. He wouldn't be surprised to see yellow snow mixed in as well.

The sky was gray. There weren't leaves on any of the trees, and they looked ugly and wet. A few days ago, they glistened as the newly fallen snow clung to all the branches, creating a beautiful, almost silver, scene. As the temperature rose slightly above freezing, that beauty melted, and the fresh silver melted away or dropped to the streets.

This was just everyday life for Kyle. If there was snow on the ground, he knew what was coming. When there wasn't snow, there would probably be a punch in the arm. A kick in groin. Either way, he was losing his milk money and would have to drink from the water fountain. He could expect to take a beating of some fashion. At the minimum, his books would be knocked from his hands, and his lunch and after-school snack would be taken. This was par for the course on his walk to school.

"Maybe today will be different," Kyle's own voice mocked him.

Kyle was gangly and pale. Red hair, freckles, crooked teeth, and glasses. Mom said God created everyone in His own image. Kyle thought God must be very odd looking or has a strange sense of humor.

Kyle always came home from school hungry and alone. He'd use the key under the mat by the back door to let himself in until his mom came home from work. He used to blame his mom for not being there to walk him to school, but deep down he knew she didn't want to go to work. They needed the extra money and her job as a secretary at Bethany College was steady. His dad's job wasn't.

Kyle loved his dad, who was a legendary high school football player in his hometown. He had scholarship offers from a lot of the big schools in the area. Everyone said that if he didn't tear up his knee in the state playoffs, he would have gone pro for sure. Instead, he lives in the same town he grew up and sold insurance. At least he did this month. He had trouble keeping a job because he drank too much. Kyle's dad spent a lot of time living off those memories of what might have been.

Dad was Kyle's hero, and he couldn't muster up the courage to tell him that he was getting beat up every day.

Kyle slowed his pace as he heard the footsteps catching up to him. A while back he had resigned himself that it was probably best to just to get it over with. One time when he tried to run, they chased him all the way to Buffalo Creek. He had hoped that he could hop across the ice and maybe his larger foes would be too heavy and fall in the icy water, sending them down stream to the ends of the earth.

No such luck that day.

"Maybe today will be different," the voice in Kyle's head told him again as he wiped his nose with his mitten.

Brian and Pauley were now just a few feet away. They were a full head taller and a year older than Kyle. Their winter coats were unzipped, and their noses were red from the cold. Neither wore a hat. Both had a snowball in each hand. Brian was tossing one a few inches in the air and catching it, taunting Kyle. As usual, there was nobody else around to defend him. None of the other kids had to take this route to school.

"Hand it over," Brian demanded as he dropped one of the snowballs and extended his arm to Kyle.

"I-I don't have any milk money today," Kyle stammered. "My mom forgot to give me some pennies this morning because she was running late for work."

Not a total lie, as his mom was indeed running late today.

Brian gave Kyle a shove, sending the younger boy reeling and doing a backwards summersault. The sack lunch fell in one direction, the books in the other direction, while his glasses fell before him in the snow.

Pauley ran over and quickly began to rifle through Kyle's coat pockets searching for coins. All he found was a handkerchief Kyle's mom stuck in there. He pulled Kyle to his feet and made him turn his pants pockets inside out.

No joy.

"Looks like you'll owe us for two days tomorrow," Brian sneered as he picked up Kyle's lunch bag.

Kyle went to pick up his books, and Pauley gave him another shove. Kyle toppled over into the wet slush.

The bullies walked off with Kyle's lunch as he stood and watched them round the corner.

Kyle bent over and pulled off his stocking cap and the five pennies dropped out: four into his hand and one into the snow. At least he could get some milk in the cafeteria today. Smiling at Abe Lincoln's chipped face as he picked the fallen penny out of the snow, he wondered if he should tell his dad about today.

Putting his cap back on, Kyle turned and continued his normal path to school. He smiled as he enjoyed his new daydream. He wished he could see Brian and Pauley eating the lunch they had stolen from him today. He wondered which would be enjoying the peanut butter and booger sandwich he had prepared, and which would be eating the container of stew that had a fresh fur ball his cat had hacked up this morning.

He smiled to himself, wiping his runny nose again with a soggy mitten.

"Today is different. Today is not the same," Kyle thought.

He raised an eyebrow as he sidestepped a fresh pile of dog poo on the sidewalk, and he wondered what special lunch he'd be making his foes tomorrow.

MARCH 1964

FORT PIERCE, FLORIDA

Charles' heart skipped a beat as he dropped into the front seat of his blue Cadillac.

"Get out, you crazy son of a bitch!" Charles said angrily as he stared at his nemesis through the rearview mirror. It had been several months since he had seen Evan. Charles thought he had given Evan the slip and didn't expect to see him. "I don't know how you got in here but get the hell out."

"Easy Charlie," Evan said. "C'mon. How long has it been? You've been ignoring me, Charlie."

Charles hated it when he called him 'Charlie.' He hated everything about Evan, even his pale blue eyes. They had met when they were both nineteen and had it out for the first time shortly after.

"Let's take a ride," Evan continued.

Although they were the same age, Evan always treated Charles as his younger subordinate.

Charles didn't turn around. Instead, he started the car, turned down the radio, and put the car in drive. He was more frustrated than afraid of Evan these days.

"I told you last time, you're not welcomed here," Charles said, glancing into the mirror.

"After all we've been through," Evan mocked. "You need me. You'd be nothing without me. How many times have I bailed you out? How many times…"

"How many times have you messed things up," Charles interrupted angrily. Loosening his thin black tie from the collar of his white shirt, which irritated the fat roles in in his neck. "You cost me my job. You cost me Sarah."

"Oh, don't blame me for that," Evan said, calmly as always. "You think you were really good enough for Sarah? You were lucky that lasted as long as it did. I know who you are, Charlie. I'll bet she's thanking me for showing her who you really are, too. Besides, she would have been in the way."

Charles was grinding his teeth as he gripped the steering wheel tightly. He wanted to grab Evan by the throat and squeeze the life out of him once and for all, but he knew he couldn't do that. He flattened his thinning black hair that was combed to the side with his hand. Staring back into the mirror Charles fought back, "That was your fault. If you hadn't shown up at the restaurant, it would have all been fine. She would have never known, and it wouldn't be an issue. I was going to ask her to marry me, eventually."

"Oh, so then you were going to tell her that nasty little secret, eh," Evan challenged. "Trust me, Charlie, it's easier this way. Now you and I can sort out what we need to sort out."

Charles glanced at the road in front of him, then back into the mirror.

"So, do you even like Florida, Charlie," Evan continued. "I mean, did you really think I wouldn't find you here?"

"You want too much from me," Charles said. "I can't give you what you want. I've told you that."

"You need to cut back on the meds," Evan mocked again. "You've been trying to get rid of me for how long now? Come on. We were great together at Fagan and DiCarlo. That place would have been nothing without us. They did us a favor by letting us go. Now look at us. We're one of the best up and coming advertising firms in the state."

"It's not 'we;' it's 'me!' I told you, you were finished six months ago," Charles seethed. "I never should have let you into the office. When I told you never to come back, I meant it!"

"I have to admit, Florida *is* growing on me," Evan said, ignoring Charles. Then his voice turned to a growl for the first time. "I think I might stay this time."

Charles was momentarily losing his resolve. He slapped the steering wheel in frustration. Seeing the sign for the toll road, he fished for change in his ash tray. A used piece of chewing gum stuck a dime and a penny together. Charles' face began to get bright red as he scraped the gum from the coin with some of it remaining lodged in the chip in Lincoln's nose on the old penny. The rest of it stuck to his fingers, causing further frustration.

"Charlie," Evan began.

"Just leave me alone," Charles spat back, still looking down at the gum on his fingers.

"Charlie, I think you should listen to me," Evan said with a little more sense of urgency.

"No, dammit!" Charles yelled as stared back into the mirror.

"Charlie, look up!" Evan shouted.

Charles looked up through his windshield only to see the red break lights of the stopped truck in front of him. He slammed on the breaks, arching his back as his arms locked straight out in front of him on the wheel. The Cadillac fishtailed slightly and came to a stop, inches from the back of the truck.

Charles put his head down. The sweat was beading on his forehead. He felt like crying. What could he do?

"See," Evan said with a noticeable sense of victory. "You still need me."

Charles raised his head to look into the mirror as his own pale blue eyes stared back at him. He didn't have to turn around to know that nobody was in the back seat, but Evan was still there. And he wasn't going anywhere.

HOT SPRINGS, SOUTH DAKOTA

The rain had stopped, at least for the moment, as soon as the red station wagon pulled into the cemetery. Five-year-old D.J. liked wearing his rain boots and slicker, so he didn't even ask if he could take them off as his mother parked the car.

D.J. liked riding by himself in the rear of the station wagon where they would put their suitcases when making long trips. This wasn't one of those trips, so he had room to spread out by himself.

Vick carried his two-year-old granddaughter, Allie, who had been sitting on his lap in the back seat, and D.J. hopped over the back seat to follow them out the door.

"Let's go see Daddy," D.J.'s mother, Macey, said as she put on a brave smile.

They walked slowly among the headstones. Macey knew where to go, but sometimes she got lost in the rows and had to check herself. She tried not to look at the names or the dates on the graves. It made her too sad.

D.J. held his mother's hand, stumbling every few steps as his face was pointed up toward the gray sky watching a bird and imagining that one cloud looked like a dinosaur.

Macey paused once and turned back to make sure she hadn't miscounted the rows. Turning left, she recognized Dewey's headstone, six places in.

Macey sighed as she brushed away some of the dirt and dead wet grass that were stuck on the marker. She was proud of her husband and missed him every day. She resented finding out about his death from a telegram. Ironically, she had received a letter from him the day before explaining how he was counting down the days until the end of his tour in Vietnam. There was no telling how long ago he requested to have it mailed.

"Can you give us a minute, Dad?" she asked Vick, who nodded with a knowing smile. Vick understood that she didn't want her children to see her break down again. Shifting Allie to his right shoulder, he took D.J.'s hand and began to lead them down the row.

D.J. couldn't help but notice the coins on his father's headstone. He had seen them before. Some had nickels. Others had dimes. Every once in a while, there was a quarter. There were a few pennies as well. Grandpa Vick told him that soldiers or even families of soldiers were leaving coins if they knew the fallen soldier or served with them in some capacity.

D.J. was always proud when he saw a bunch of different coins on his father's headstone. He told Grandpa Vick that it meant his daddy must have had lots of friends. D.J., or Dewey, Jr., was a lot like his dad.

A light drizzle began to fall again. Vick let go of D.J.'s hand, so he could open his umbrella and keep the three of them covered. He knew D.J. didn't mind getting a little wet. Besides, he had his favorite yellow slicker and rain boots on.

"Quack, quack, quack," D.J. chirped as he flapped his arms, pretending he was a duck.

"Shhhhh," Vick said with his index finger to his lips, which were curved upward in a smile.

D.J. acknowledged by quacking in a whisper a few more times. He stopped in front of a lonely grave. There were no flowers, and no coins.

"What does it say, Grandpa?" D.J. asked.

"Corporal Tyler Reagan," Vick squinted through the rain drops.

D.J. looked up at his grandfather, who smiled and knew what he wanted. He fished out a pocket full of pennies and placed them in D.J.'s hand. The five-year-old carefully took one and placed it on top of Corporal Reagan's stone.

They meandered through the rows with Vick looking back every once in a while, to check on Macey. D.J. would stop at any grave that he thought looked "lonely" and pay his respects with a penny. Vick would call out the name of the fallen soldier because D.J. wanted to know their names. They did this on every visit.

"If you see my Daddy, tell him I miss him," D.J. told a private named Reed Madison as the rain fell harder.

Vick always marveled at D.J.'s handling of his father's death in Vietnam. He cried from time to time, but he seemed to take a responsibility of putting on a brave face for his mother. Maybe he was just too young to really understand.

D.J. noticed another woman in a black coat three rows away. Her eyes were closed as she stood in front of another grave. He wanted to look and see if there were any coins on the headstone, but he decided the woman would probably take care of that if she was visiting someone she knew.

The rain began pouring heavily, and Vick was a little concerned about his daughter, so he steered D.J. back in her direction. She had opened her own umbrella, but kneeling on one knee, her plaid pants were getting soaked.

Vick shifted Allie to his other shoulder again as D.J. skipped behind him. Vick could see his daughter's eyes were red from crying. Right on cue, D.J. skipped into her arms, wrapping his own arms around her neck in the perfect embrace.

Releasing his mom, D.J.'s eyebrows arched upward, and his tongue was pressed against his bottom lip and chin. A look that was asking for permission.

D.J. took the last penny and placed it on his father's stone. Abraham Lincoln's chipped nose was hit by a fat rain drop.

"Happy birthday, Daddy," D.J. whispered.

As they walked back to the car, the rain stopped as quickly as it started.

D.J. looked skyward again. Sun beams appearing through a small break in the clouds shone on the cemetery, seemingly holding back the dark clouds behind them, just for a moment.

The family climbed into the red station wagon and pulled out of the cemetery to head home. Looking out the back window, D.J. looked for pictures in the gray clouds and imagined he saw a smiling man with long hair. In his mind, it was the face of God.

A cleansing rain began again, washing away the grass and dirt on the rows of headstones.

SOMEWHERE OVER ARKANSAS

It was her head slamming against the side of the plane that woke Angie up from her nap, but the simultaneous screams of the passengers a second later as the American Airlines 727 had quickly dropped one hundred feet would have done the trick as well.

"Jesus!" Angie said out loud as she turned to the stranger in the seat next to her.

"Turbulence," the young businessman named Aaron said nervously, while trying but failing to sound like he wasn't rattled. "Like a speed bump."

"No shit," an annoyed passenger in the row ahead of them said.

As Angie opened the shade of her window, Aaron reluctantly peered out. He half expected to see a creature on the wing which would suddenly press its face against the window at the next lightning strike. The former did not happen, but the latter did.

The white flash of lightening sounded like a small explosion that shook the plane again.

The jet seemed to settle and find smooth air for a moment. A father and son across the aisle resumed their game of penny-ante blackjack on their tray table.

"I'm betting $1,943," the preteen boy said as he slid his penny with the 1943 D date. "Hit me."

Right on cue the jet seemed to hit another "speed bump" as it rapidly made another sudden drop in altitude. The cards flew in the air as did the coins on the table, led by the sixteenth president's imperfect nose.

Other passengers lost their drinks in the aisle, all at once. The plane quickly looked like a teenage house party when the parents leave town. It was shaking at an increasingly alarming and violent rate, but no one wanted to be at this party.

The pilot tried making an announcement, but nobody could make out what he was saying over the rattling and the din of the passengers.

Aaron realized he was holding his breath and slowly exhaled. The thirty-year-old had been on plenty of bumpy flights, but this was beyond anything he had ever experienced.

Angie had closed her eyes. The twenty-eight-year-old was saying a silent prayer. She could feel the early signs of a panic attack trying to take control as the aircraft continued to rattle and dip. Her heart was pounding in her chest, and she started thinking about all the mistakes in her life and the things she had not done yet. Find a man. Get married. Kids. She was brushing her wavy brown hair with her hand with no apparent purpose.

Aaron could see that his seatmate was coming unglued, and he wasn't doing much better. He just then realized how cute the young woman was, even wearing a face of sheer terror.

For a brief moment, Aaron forgot his fear. "Why hadn't I noticed her earlier?" he wondered.

More turbulence brought him back to the reality of the situation. He reflexively placed his hand over Angie's on the shared armrest between them. Angie opened her eyes and slowly turned her head in his direction.

Aaron wasn't sure if she thought he did it as a calming gesture to her, or if she knew he was scared, too. Or maybe she thought he was hitting on her at a very inappropriate time.

All three scenarios crossed his brain simultaneously.

Previously, the nose of the plane had arched upward, as if the pilot was trying to fly above the storm they were passing through. Now it was clearly pointed downward.

A flash of orange interrupted the white flashes of lightening in the dark sky, causing Aaron to squeeze Angie's hand tighter than he or she wanted.

"Do you mind if I close the window," he said with his voice shaking. He didn't actually wait for an answer, but he didn't want Angie to see the flames now coming out of the engine on the wing.

"The plane's on fire!" someone screamed from two rows back. "We're gonna die!"

"So much for that," Aaron thought.

Screams erupted from all parts of the aircraft even though the flaming engine had extinguished itself quickly.

"Ladies and gentlemen, we're going to have to make an emergency landing. Please make sure your seat belt is…" the captain's voice was cut off after another huge "speed bump" rocked the cabin.

More screams.

More prayers.

Angie was beating herself up inside for all the stupid things she wasted time stressing about that really didn't matter.

The plane began to descend at a steeper angle. Angie and Aaron looked at each other, each thinking the same thought, "Are we going to crash?"

The jet wavered back and forth. Aaron could picture the pilots struggling with the yolk, like the bomber pilots in the old World War II movies. He didn't realize how hard he was squeezing Angie's hand until she finally wrestled it free due to the pain.

Angie had broken out into a noticeable cold sweat. All over. All at once.

Drink cups and soda cans rolled on the floor.

After what seemed like hours but was actually only minutes, the jet broke free of the dark clouds. Its nose was still pointed downward and now Angie was sure they were going to die. Right there. Right then.

She flung the window shade open again and was surprised to see the lights of the land below. They were getting closer and larger, rapidly.

The plane continued to shutter, and it wasn't getting level yet.

Inside the cockpit the pilot and copilot were struggling. The copilot, Rick, suggested that they were going to have to abort the landing due to severe cross winds and try again.

Understanding the risk, Captain Erickson, overruled. "We'll never make it and have to ditch if we don't take it down right now. My call."

As the plane continued to rapidly lose altitude, it was clear to Angie, Aaron, and everyone else aboard that coming out of the storm had not gotten them out of the woods. The plane appeared to be failing.

Across the aisle, the father was holding his arm around his terrified son. Both had tears coming down their faces.

OXFORD, MISSISSIPPI

The rainwater trickled down Van Buren Avenue, puddling in various places on the cracked sidewalk. Horace stared straight ahead, hands in the pockets of his black wool coat. His black skin ashen with the cool November air, he felt the cold on the top of his head. He cursed himself for not bringing his wool cap. He should know better. Growing up in Mississippi, he knew that as hot as it was during the summer and fall months, there were occasionally cold spells in the winter.

Even though he had lived outside of Detroit for the better part of the last five years, the memories of growing up in the Deep South had built his character to this point. Walking these streets as a child in the 1940s could always be difficult. It was better now to a certain extent, but old habits die hard.

As he passed the First Baptist Church on his right, his eyes took him back in time. He was six years old the first time he remembered being called "nigger," and he didn't like it. He didn't like the word, nor how it was said. Horace and his brothers had been walking back from the old negro church a few blocks away on Jackson Avenue, and while passing the First Baptist Church on their way home, he heard it.

"Nappy-headed bunch of niggers," the large man in a gray suit and black tie said. The man had his hands on his hips and was ironically standing beside a hand-made sign in front of the church which read, "*Love thy neighbor.*"

Horace didn't really know what the word meant at the time, but he knew he didn't like it based on the disdain in the man's voice. He would always say that was the moment he first wanted to do something to create change. He grew up angry, but scared. As he became older, he was able to channel that rage he felt inside with a sense of purpose as he later walked with Dr. Martin Luther King in Selma, Alabama.

With his mind still drifting in the past, Horace turned his head back up the road and continued his walk. Now in his early forties, he looked much older. His hair was receding in the front and showing signs of gray.

The sound of footsteps moving faster than his caused him to turn around. A man in a blue winter coat and orange hunting cap with ear flaps was walking an Irish Setter and gaining ground. The dog was pulling hard on the leash and growled at each car that passed on the road. Horace's body tensed reflexively, but he turned his eyes forward convincing himself he would be fine. The man and the dog passed moments later, taking a bit of an elliptical route around Horace without incident.

The image of teenagers taunting him by chasing him with their dogs those many years ago haunted him for a moment, but the sound of a fire engine somewhere in the distance brought his eyes back to the present.

Further up Van Buren Avenue he passed the First Presbyterian Church, thinking about the funeral of his grandfather for which he had returned to Mississippi. Everywhere he turned, he saw ghosts from his childhood. Not all of the memories were bad. After all, this was home.

Reaching the town square, Horace stepped over an old broken bourbon bottle, then paused to stare at the LaFayette County Courthouse. The American flag flew on one flagpole, while the Confederate battle flag flew on another.

Horace took one lap around the square just to see all the shops that he remembered and to see what others had been replaced with something new. He stared in the windows, not realizing he was smiling for some reason until he caught his own reflection in the department store window. After satisfying his curiosity he stopped into a café he was not allowed to enter as a child.

The white-haired waitress offered a menu as he sat at a table next to the wall. Her right arm bent to the right, away from her body, with an unfiltered cigarette burning between her index and middle fingers. The cigarette was badly in need of a tapping with a full inch of ash dangling from the end.

"Just coffee," Horace said staring at the cigarette.

He stared out the window and watched the people come and go while sipping his coffee. The muffled sounds of conversation, tinkling of silverware on plates, and fuzzy chatter of country music coming across the AM radio on the counter were all unheard by Horace as again his eyes took him back in time. He remembered the protests when the university, known to everyone simply as "Ole Miss," was integrated in 1962 and how Governor Ross Barnett said that no Mississippi school would be integrated while he was in office. "Why was everyone so angry?" he remembered thinking.

Horace paid for his coffee and counted his change as he walked toward the door to leave. A pretty young white girl with light brown hair, probably a college student, held the door open for him with one hand while holding a book by Faulkner in the other.

"After you, Sir," she said with an honest smile.

He stared for a moment at the penny in his hand with Lincoln's chipped nose, glanced at the orange and blue flag waving in the town square, and chuckled at the irony.

Thanking the young lady, Horace smiled and decided he knew where he'd walk next: campus.

Horace never went to college, but he was educated.

BALDWIN, MICHIGAN

"What the hell is she doing here," Nathan thought to himself. He had really only come into the church to get warm; then found himself praying for the first time in many years. He had sort of given up on God because he thought God had given up on him.

Nathan hadn't noticed that he had closed his eyes until the first members of the congregation had filed in for the service. It was warm in the church, so he decided to stay as more worshipers found their place. Nathan didn't know it was Sunday. Living out of his car for the last two weeks, he had lost track of everything. At thirty-eight and homeless for the first time in his life, he didn't think he could sink much lower. His wife left him a year ago for another man. That led to the drinking, drinking at work, and then missing work. It didn't take long for him to lose his job, and he just stopped caring about himself and his responsibilities. The bank foreclosed on his house when he stopped making payments.

It was getting harder and harder to get part time work to keep money in his pocket. Nathan had recently humbled himself to shower at the homeless shelter but wouldn't dare sleep there.

"What the hell is she doing here," he said to himself again. Allison hadn't aged much at all and seeing her sent him back to a different time.

It had been nearly two decades since he saw Allison back in their hometown of Albion, but she was instantly recognizable to him. Nathan had a school-boy crush on her since the fourth grade. He didn't work up the courage to ask her out for a movie and a soda until the eighth grade, but he ended up getting the flu the next day and his mother made him cancel. He never worked up the courage to ask again. In high school, she started dating the captain of the football team, who was two years ahead of them. She went off to college at Butler, and he had heard she got married a short time later.

Nathan was suddenly ashamed of what he had become and tried to make himself smaller. He wanted to leave, but there was something in his soul that tugged at him to stay so he could stare at her longer. She was three rows ahead of him and across the aisle, but he thought if he got up to leave, she might notice and recognize him. There were now parishioners on either side of him in the pew, although they were a few feet away. He suddenly became very aware that he hadn't showered in a couple of days.

Feeling the scraggly facial hair that he had allowed to grow the last two weeks; he was even more uncomfortable.

A small choir made up mostly of women and young teenagers filed in and began to sing.

Nathan's mind began to wander. He wondered how his life would have been different if he hadn't caught the flu all those years ago, or maybe if he had worked up the courage to ask her out again. Now it was too late. There she was, beautiful as ever. He assumed the well-dressed man with her was her husband. He was clean-shaven and his gray suit fit perfectly.

The pastor was well into his sermon, and Nathan was sure he couldn't get up to leave now. Surely God was having a good laugh about this pauper who didn't come to worship and was now torturing him with his forgotten love. Nathan felt as if all the eyes of the churchgoers were upon him.

He looked around to see that wasn't the case, however. The older couple to his left were intently listening. They were both well-groomed. The family to his right was a slice of apple pie with a pre-teen son using his fingers to comb his feathered hair. The younger daughter twirled her brown hair in her fingers and smiled at Nathan.

Averting his gaze, the twenty-something man in front of him was less formally dressed and had his arm around his pregnant wife.

As he studied more of the people in the church, Nathan found some comfort. He became aware of those that weren't paying attention and some that weren't attired in their Sunday best. He started to relax a little bit.

He watched Allison watch the man at the lectern, who was telling a story of a beggar who was hoping to get scraps from the master's table. It was hard for Nathan to pay attention.

"Where did I go wrong?" Nathan mused as his gaze found the crucifix at the front of the church. He regretted not being more adventurous and never leaving Michigan to see what else was out there. He regretted marrying Elaine because he felt like it was time to settle down, regardless of whether he truly loved her, and she, him. He regretted the choices he had made that led him to this moment. For a moment, he even regretted coming into the church to get warm. Most of all, he regretted not calling on Allison after he recovered from the flu.

His self-loathing was interrupted as the collection plate was placed before him. Reflexively, he pulled out his wallet and pulled out two of his remaining six dollars. Before he realized what he was doing, and with his eyes transfixed again on Allison, his left hand toppled the collection held loosely by his pew neighbor. The contents flew six inches in the air, some of the coins clattered loudly on the pew in front of him.

Snapping out of his trance, Nathan quickly swept the floor with his hands, picking up the dollars, envelopes, and coins to put them back in the plate. The warm rush of blood to his face was immediate as he blushed a bright red.

The older man next to him held the plate, as Nathan scraped the last remaining coins from the pew. He again wanted to make himself small and hide behind the dirty penny with part of Abraham Lincoln's nose missing.

Finally passing the plate to his right, Nathan bravely tilted his head upward. Allison was now staring at him as if staring right through him. Dozens of thoughts collided with Nathan's brain at once.

"Did she recognize me? Was that a look of shame or empathy? Was she upset that I disturbed the service?"

Nathan felt a chill and a warm flash through his body simultaneously. Most of his body was now damp with a cool sweat as he looked away from his long-lost love. He glanced back a moment later to find that she was trained on what was happening up front once again.

He didn't move for the rest of the service and couldn't wait to get out of there.

As the final hymn was being sung, Nathan slipped out of the pew, excusing himself as he passed the older couple who didn't appreciate the interruption of Amazing Grace.

The echoes of the choir were still in his ears as he shuffled quickly through the parking lot, fumbled through his pockets for his keys and unlocked the door for his blue Chevy Nova. Taking his seat, he could see the parishioners starting to make their way out of the church.

Nathan turned the key in the ignition to make his getaway.

Nothing.

He tried again.

Nothing.

This had happened before and Nathan knew he had to replace a cable of some sort, but he just couldn't afford it. He wanted to crawl into his backseat and hide until everyone left but realized there were cars parked on either side of him. Surely, they would see him as they got into their cars.

Nathan popped the hood, hoping he could quickly jiggle the wires and make his getaway. He held the hood open with his left hand, using his right hand to shake the offending cable. Satisfied it would work, he dropped the hood.

And there she was.

"Nathan Michaels, is that you?" Allison said as she stood between him and his front door.

Nathan stood silent for a moment, the blood rushing back into his face again. He wanted to run. He wanted to hug her. He wanted to say something fantastic, but all his brain would allow to escape was, "Hi."

"I knew that was you. I just knew it!" Allison said, moving forward and giving him a warm embrace.

Nathan's muscles froze for a moment and then allowed him to awkwardly return the hug. He wanted to squeeze her and hold on. He also wanted to run away.

"Allison. Wow! What a surprise," Nathan stammered. "Gosh, how long has it been?"

"I knew it was you. See, Tommy, I told you that's who it was," she said, turning to the man who had accompanied her. "Nathan, do you remember my brother, Tommy? I'm here visiting Tommy and his family. His wife and daughter are in the choir."

"Oh, your brother? Yes, sure," Nathan stumbled as he shook Tommy's hand. "The music was beautiful."

"Thanks," Tommy replied. "I'm going to go back in and see if I can drag my family away from the post-church gossip, and you two can catch up for a minute."

Allison smiled a beautiful smile at Nathan, and he realized that she was not at all disgusted by his appearance. His shoulders relaxed as he tried to think of something to say, but she made it easy for him.

"I haven't been back to Michigan since my divorce. You know how it is in the Midwest, a divorce makes you the black sheep of the family," she chuckled.

"Don't I know it," Nathan thought, marveling at how full of energy she was.

"This is so great!" she beamed. "Hey, you know what? I'll go tell Tommy to meet us in town in about a half hour at the diner, so we can get out of the cold and chat. That's if, I'm not keeping you from anything?

"Uh, no. That would be great," Nathan said, smiling for the first time in nearly a year.

"Great! You owe me a date anyway," Allison winked as she turned to catch her brother. "Let's go get that soda."

CEDAR RAPIDS, IOWA

Edwin was biting down so hard on his tongue, it hurt. He had to do something to keep from laughing or even smiling. The ten-year-old was trying to keep his body from shaking as well.

He wasn't alone in his predicament. Every boy in the fifth-grade class at St. Pius Elementary was doing something similar.

Edwin knew today would be tough because he had been reading ahead in his textbooks, only to discover that today was *the* day. His older brother, Kevin, had warned him about it before. It was the day the class learned about the birds and the bees. Sister Frances Marie would be reading about sex education directly from the textbook. Kevin had warned him not to laugh or so much as snicker or smile, lest you feel the wrath of Sister Frances Marie.

And so, it began.

The rest of the boys in his class were educated on how to act as well, but that didn't mean they'd all get through it un-scathed.

The first time Sister Frances Marie said "penis," Edwin thought he might wet himself. After all, Sister Frances Marie had to be eighty, and she just said, "penis."

The little old woman sat there at her desk in her habit. She would pause after each paragraph and look around the room to check the faces of the children.

Edwin and his classmates had already heard plenty of other terms for the various sexual organs, but somehow it was funnier when the proper biological names were used, especially by an eighty-year-old nun.

Edwin was in the third of five rows, but he felt like Sister Frances Marie was looking directly at him at every pause.

He looked to his left, and Sherrie, the girl with the curly brown hair was stone-faced, totally unfazed. Emboldened, he looked to his right at his buddy, Doug McDonald.

Big mistake.

Doug had the book propped straight up on the desk to try to obscure his face. He had his left hand over his mouth, covering what was sure to be a huge grin. He was nearly in tears trying to hold back laughter. This made Edwin's stomach ripple and a laugh almost escaped, but somehow, he was able to correct it so that it sounded more like a cough.

Sister Frances Marie cast an eye in his direction. He could feel his face flush red, but he remained in proper character. Fear is a powerful thing.

Edwin carefully slid his book upward as he tried to mask his own face. Just in time, too, as Sister Frances Marie was describing the changes in female anatomy which included the growth of breasts.

"Oh my God!" Edwin thought. "She just said, 'breasts!'"

Thinking it couldn't get any worse, it did.

"Herman?" Sister Frances Marie said. "Why don't you read the next paragraph for us."

Poor Herman. If there was ever a poster child for attention deficit disorder, it was Herman. In this case it might not have been bad initially because Herman was off in La-La Land and probably didn't even hear Sister Frances Marie say "penis" or "breasts."

The temporary life-saving affliction would certainly be

short-lived as now Sister Frances Marie was picking students to read the remainder of the chapter.

"Oh, geez," Edwin thought. He eyed the clock, pleading with the minutes to move faster, but recess was still ten minutes away.

"Herman!" Sister Frances Marie said a second time, this time a few octaves louder. "Third paragraph on page eight."

"God, help him. God, help me!" Edwin prayed.

Herman began reading. He wasn't a great reader. His sentences were always choppy and sometimes he had to sound out long words.

Herman was now giving a lesson on the start of procreation. Hearing Herman clinically describe blood flow to male private parts was going off without a hitch, but then Edwin realized that since she was no longer reading, Sister Frances Marie could pay more attention to the individual faces around the classroom.

Edwin kept his head still but searched the room with his eyes. All the girls were handling the information like champs. Not a snicker among them.

Lizzy seemed the most studious of any of them. She had come back from summer vacation with a full set of breasts that Edwin and his buddies couldn't help but notice. Something had certainly happened between fourth and fifth grade that Edwin and the guys didn't fully understand. She now filled out the Catholic school uniform, and in gym class, Edwin couldn't help but stare when she was doing jumping jacks.

Edwin eyed the clock again. "Did time just go backwards?"

Herman had moved on to a new paragraph. The choppiness of his reading made it easier to handle the sensitive material, but then it happened. Herman stumbled on how to pronounce a word.

"Vah-guy-nuh? Vuh-," he stumbled.

"Vagina," Sister Francis Marie said to correct him.

"Oh, God," Edwin thought.

"Vuh-jye-nia," Herman tried to sound out.

"Vagina," Sister Francis Marie said again.

"Oh, God!" Edwin said to himself again as he fought his stomach's urge to produce laughter.

"Vagina," Herman said proudly, now satisfied that he had said it correctly.

Doug emitted the tiniest of snorts, and Edwin again made the mistake of looking over. A snot bubble had escaped Doug's nose on his last attempt to hold back laughter. It was all over his face. Doug frantically dug through his pockets for a tissue.

Edwin returned his gaze to Sister Frances Marie, who was now staring at Doug with one eyebrow razed. Edwin always thought she looked like Mr. Spock from Star Trek when she did that, and it temporarily kept him distracted.

As Herman finished the paragraph, Sister Frances Marie asked him to stop, and she scanned the room for the next victim to pick up the reading.

"Please God, not me, not me," Edwin prayed.

All the boys in the class had their heads down, avoiding eye contact with Sister Frances Marie. The girls seemed more well prepared. Nina even had her hand up, begging to be called upon.

Edwin and his friends always called Nina a "brown-noser," and that nickname wouldn't be lost anytime soon.

Sister Frances Marie chose Heather instead. Heather wasn't a great reader, either.

"Was she doing this on purpose?" Edwin thought.

Heather was better than Herman, but she was very soft spoken and sat in the last row. She picked up where Herman left off.

Edwin knew he couldn't take much more. He needed a distraction, even if it meant losing his place and risk being scolded if he was called to read and didn't know where they were. He pulled the penny from his pocket and tried to focus on every detail. He wondered how the chip arrived on President Lincoln's nose as he attempted to tune out Heather. He wondered what life was like in 1943. Did Sister Frances Marie teach sex education way back then?

Heather was now stumbling over a word.

"Ejaculate," Sister Francis Marie corrected.

"Oh God!" Edwin thought.

She said it again, and so did Heather. Edwin wasn't sure he could contain himself much longer.

The awkwardness was broken by Mr. Cicchinni opening up the classroom door, causing Edwin to drop his penny on the tiled floor, where it rolled silently toward Sister Frances Marie's desk.

The little Italian janitor always walked straight in while making his rounds, regardless of who was teaching what in every classroom. The teachers had become used to his interruptions because he always greeted them with a polite, "Hallo," in heavy Italian-accented English.

This was Edwin's "out" to allow a soft giggle, along with several others in the class because they always giggled when he entered.

Clad in his green cardigan sweater and blue jeans, he grabbed the waste basket and the penny that now lay next to it and exited.

Edwin frowned at the loss of his funds and needed distraction as Heather began to read again softly.

"Louder," Sister Francis Marie corrected.

Heather repeated the previous sentence as Edwin went back to biting his tongue. He couldn't handle much more, and then Sister Frances Marie stopped her from reading as she finished the paragraph.

"Edwin," she called out.

"Was that a smile on her face?" Edwin wondered as he looked up at the old nun. He was terrified and not because he didn't know where they were in the reading. This was the summary part where he would have to say all those words at once!

Doug was still wiping snot from his nose and leaned his head forward so Edwin could see it, as if to say, "You're dead, buddy!"

Edwin took a deep breath. "Chapter summary."

The loud buzzing sound stopped him in his tracks. That was the bell to end class. All the boys stood up as quickly as they could to get out of class and hit the playground for recess.

Sister Frances Marie held up her hand to quiet everyone. Looking at Edwin, she announced that they would pick up where they left off tomorrow.

Edwin was already thinking about which sickness to fake in order to miss school.

SEATTLE, WASHINGTON

Benny let out a short squeal as his father pulled the brown Chevy Impala into the parking lot of the Kingdome.

"Whoa," Benny said before turning to look at his father. "Is that where the Mariners really play baseball?"

Jack smiled at his youngest son and nodded his head. The Mariners were playing in only their second season as a Major League Baseball club, and not playing well, but it was Benny's first game. Everything was magical.

"I can't believe this. I can't believe we're here!" Benny said over and over.

Father and son exited the car and held hands as they made their way through the parking lot to enter the stadium. Benny kept adjusting his Mariners hat that Jack had bought for him on his birthday. That's when he gave him the tickets, too.

Benny wasn't an athlete by any stretch of the imagination. He couldn't throw very well, and he couldn't catch, but he didn't care. Benny loved baseball. He loved to watch it with his dad on television. It didn't matter which team was playing. Sometimes he would listen to the games on the radio and cheer when his favorite player got a hit. He'd make his dad read him the stories in the newspaper every morning about the previous night's game.

Benny collected baseball cards and took his time to separate them by teams. He didn't understand everything about the game, and Jack would often have to repeat the rules and why things were happening.

It had been ten days since Benny received the tickets for his birthday. Every morning since, he would walk to his parent's bedroom upon waking up and ask, "Is tonight the night?"

Tonight *was* the night. Benny couldn't contain himself all day.

As they walked through the concourse, Benny's senses were overloaded with sights and smells he had never imagined. For a moment, he forgot he was at a baseball game.

"How about a hot dog?" Jack asked.

Benny nodded and smiled as they entered the que. He pulled out his rubber change purse, intending to pay for his meal, fishing out a nickel and two pennies.

"I got this, Benny," his father chuckled. "This is my treat, remember?"

Benny nodded, staring at his funny penny with a little piece dug out of President Lincoln's face. He thought about saving it because it was different, but decided it was just as a good as any other penny.

"I'll get the tip!" Benny said as he put his money down next to his father's.

Father and son held hands once again as they descended the steps to their seats. Benny stopped after two steps, looking up from his hot dog to see the wonder displayed before him. This huge arena with lights and a turf field was the most wondrous thing he had ever seen.

Benny turned to look at his father, a piece of hot dog hanging out of his mouth as he stopped chewing while taking in the view.

Jack laughed and was taken aback, remembering when his father took him to his first baseball game in New York. It was a long time ago, but he remembered the joy in his own heart. Seeing that joy in his son made this experience even better than his own.

They continued down the steps, and Benny adjusted his hat with the half-eaten hot dog in his hand, spreading some mustard on the side of it.

Benny couldn't believe how close they were getting to the field. His eyes got bigger with each step they took. There were hundreds of conversations happening at once all around them.

"This is us," Jack said as they reached the front row beside the third base dugout, which was occupied by the Mariners.

Benny started hopping up and down, clapping his hands and then holding his face in pure ecstasy. He could almost reach out and touch the players he would see on TV and on his baseball cards.

Father and son took their seats and Benny stared into the dugout. He waved at a player who happened to be looking his way. The player waved back. Benny laughed, almost to the point of tears and waved again.

Benny sat in his seat and pounded his baseball glove with his other hand, signifying that he was ready for action. He saw the guys on the field do it, so he figured he looked good.

As the National Anthem was about to be played, Jack told Benny to remove his hat and hold his hand on his heart. Benny didn't know all the words, but he tried to hum the tune while others sang.

"Who are the Mariners playing today, Dad?" Benny asked.

"Look over into the other dugout across the field," Jack said, pointing to the first base dugout. "It's the Twins. The Minnesota Twins."

"I hope the Mariners win," Benny said, clamping his hands together as if to pray.

Things didn't look good early. The Twins scored three runs in the first inning. Benny was sad, but Jack reminded him that there were nine innings, and the Mariners haven't even been up to bat yet.

Benny composed himself and stood up when the first Mariner batter went to the plate.

"Come on guys!" He yelled. "It's my first game!"

The Mariners responded, not necessarily to Benny's plea, but they rallied, nonetheless. After scoring twice in the bottom of the first, they loaded the bases in the second inning and Leon Roberts hit a three-run double to put the home team on top.

"Go, go, go, go!" Benny screamed as each runner crossed the plate.

The rest of the night belonged to the Mariners. It wasn't easy for Benny to keep up with the game with all the sounds and sights. He didn't complain, though. He just took it all in. Jack reeled him back in when the Mariners loaded the bases in the fifth inning.

"That means we have a runner on every base," Jack instructed. "Do you know what happens if this guy hits a home run? It's a grand slam."

Right on cue, Bob Stinson clubbed the next pitch over the left field wall, and Benny nearly lost his mind.

"Dad, you did it!" Benny squealed.

Jack laughed and hugged his son.

A few innings later, Benny was thirsty, so Jack flagged down one of the concessionaires for a couple of sodas. Benny clapped his hands excitedly. He was only allowed to drink soda on special occasions.

A few minutes later, Benny was determined to slurp the last remaining drops of his soda through the ice in his cup. He hadn't noticed the crack of the bat and everyone around him standing up as the foul ball approached.

"Watch out, Benny," Jack shouted as the third baseman came running over to try to make the play.

Larry Wolfe of the Twins leaned over the rail to make the catch, nearly six inches from Benny's head. For his part, Benny didn't even flinch. He was still focused on moving the ice in his cup and sucking the last bit of soda through his straw.

The third baseman looked at Benny. "Hey, buddy."

Benny looked up as the visiting player held out the ball and nodded. Benny took the ball out of his hand, not really understanding what just happened.

He looked at his father, and then looked into the dugout where one of the Mariners had turned towards him and was smiling.

"Is this your ball?" Benny asked, motioning as if he was going to throw it to him.

"No, you can keep it!" the player said with a smile.

Benny's mouth dropped as he started hugging the baseball as if it were his favorite teddy bear. His attention span lagged most of the remainder of the game, but that was fine for Jack. He was happy for this memory and hoped Benny would remember it, too.

After nearly three hours, the final out was made. The Mariners won and an exhausted Benny was leaning against his father's shoulder. He was emotionally drained from his first baseball game. Jack held his arm around his son and the fans behind them filed out.

The players gathered their gloves, gum, tobacco, and sunflower seeds from the dugout. Benny turned his head for one last look into where his heroes lived. The player he "met" earlier smiled and gave him another wave. Benny smiled back and waved once more.

Jack struggled to his feet. The sixty-seven-year-old retiree from the city water department, kissed the top of his forty-year-old Down syndrome son's head. "Time to go, buddy."

Father and son held hands as they walked up the steps and into the night with a baseball in Benny's glove, and a lifetime of memories in Jack's head.

STAMFORD, CONNECTICUT

"Twenty-five cents," the man behind the counter, known only as "Joe" said to the red-haired boy looking up at him.

Connor fished the coin out of his pocket to pay for his pack of Topps baseball cards. The eleven-year-old bounced out of Joe's Corner Store, down the two concrete steps, and pulled on the door to the back seat of the wood-paneled station wagon. Before he could slide into his mom's car beside his eight-year-old brother Scotty, his eyes caught an old penny. Abraham Lincoln looked up from the faded sweltering pavement.

"Be right back," he called to his mom who was singing along with Captain and Tennille on the AM radio.

It didn't take Connor more than a second to scoop up the penny. He rubbed the 1943 D bronze beauty, not noticing the slight chip in Lincoln's nose. Racing back into "Joe's," he grabbed a piece of Bazooka Joe bubble gum from the bucket by the register and laid his newly found treasure down. Joe, who was shaving roast beef for Mrs. Kawalski from his deli station simply nodded as the skinny boy popped back out as quickly as he had entered, nearly bumping into a man in faded blue jeans and a sweat stained white t-shirt.

Mrs. Kawalski, a tad overweight in her late forties, didn't seem to notice as she stood in her tennis outfit. The sunburn on her arms matched her nose and forehead.

Stopping to pull up his white socks with the blue stripes, Connor felt the New England summer humidity radiating off the pavement once again on this first day of June. He stuffed the gum in his mouth while reading the short comic and fortune in the wrapper.

In true big brother fashion, he discarded the wrapper by tossing it at Scotty who was too busy rifling through his pack of baseball cards in the hopes of finding a Yankee.

"Do you wanna flip when we get home?" Connor said, referring to the little game he and his brother played whereby they could win each other's baseball cards depending on which position was listed on the individual's card.

"OK, but no Yankees," Scotty replied. He chirped as the last card in his pack revealed one of his heroes. "Bucky Dent!"

Connor fished through his cards, finding only a Thurmon Munson, the soon to be late Yankee catcher, but none from his favorite team, the Boston Red Sox.

"Oh, I'll trade ya," Scotty wailed and held up the Jim Rice card he found earlier in his back. "I got this guy."

Connor chomped the hard Bazooka Joe bubble gum, stuffed the cardboard textured gum from his baseball cards into his mouth as well and without saying a word swapped the two major league all-stars.

Who would have known that twenty-three years later, Connor would be involved in a similar but more lucrative process as an agent for players on both of those teams?

The yellow and wood-paneled station wagon, pulled onto the main road, heading east.

Inside the store, Joe had finished slicing the pound of roast beef for Mrs. Kawalski, slipped the penny still lying on the counter in the drawer and rang her up.

She was the last face Joe would remember that day.

Seven minutes later, the man in the faded blue jeans and white t-shirt with the stocking over his face hopped back into the orange Datsun 240z he had stolen thirty minutes prior. He headed west on High Ridge Road. Elvis Costello sang "Pump it up" on the AM radio.

Joe stared at his empty register. Not a single penny was left in the drawer.

WOODSTOCK, VERMONT

The daredevil waved to the crowd at the bottom of the hill. He'd be a legend if he hit the jump and landed successfully. Nobody else had the guts for this, especially not Randall's biggest rival, Victor VanDerveer.

Randall remembered when Victor broke the record, and the echo of the crowd's chant of "Victor! Victor!" haunted his dreams. The thought of himself being the one receiving the cheers and the slaps on the back drove him to this day.

Today would be *his* day. If he survived, of course. There was no turning back now.

Randall looked up to the sky overhead. Puffy white clouds and sunshine. No wind. All was perfect.

He inspected his wheels one last time as he circled his magnificent instrument of speed. Surely, he would make it across the great divide. Randall had also inspected the ramp himself carefully before ascending the steep incline he had climbed many times before. All was ready.

"Stay straight and go fast," Randall said to himself.

He pulled his helmet over his thick brown hair and clicked the chin strap. Turning his goggles toward his face, his blue eyes darted back and forth. The "Team USA" logo on the front of his helmet was centered perfectly, and he liked the way he looked in his red, white, and blue outfit.

Randall adjusted the goggles over his helmet again. He pulled on the left glove, then the right, just as he always had done. He straddled his machine and waved again to the eager crowd below before sinking into the seat.

Nick, his trusty companion, and best friend, for his whole life stepped to his side.

"Are you ready?" Nick asked.

"Let's go," Randall said, giving his friend a thumbs-up. "Light it up!"

The crowd began to chant his name over and over again.

Gripping the handlebars, he started his descent. He was picking up speed, but would it be enough? Randall kept his eyes straight ahead, locking in on the ramp below.

One-third of the way down, Randall was really moving now. He had never gone this fast before. The wind whistled through the ear holes of his helmet.

Halfway down, Randall was momentarily uncomfortable with how fast he was going.

"What if I wipe out?" he thought. "Should I pull the brake a little bit?"

His grip on the handlebars was as tight as his resolve to stick this jump.

"Randall! Randall!" came the chant from below.

Then he heard his mother cry out.

"Randall, time for lunch," she yelled from the front porch of the house near the bottom of the hill.

The sound of his mother's voice made him twitch for a moment.

He didn't hit the ramp perfectly straight. In fact, he was slightly angled, but his speed catapulted the six-year old's Big Wheel forward over the plywood ramp.

Everything else happened in slow motion.

While air-born, the bottle rockets Nick had lit and placed

in the lunch bucket behind the seat flew backwards up the hill. Randall's feet flew off the pedals attached to the large front wheel as he retained a tight grip on the plastic handlebars, streamers flailing.

The orange and yellow plastic three-wheeler soared over the chalk-drawn lines in alternating colors below.

Randall landed hard on the graying asphalt sending the coins in the pocket of his blue shorts spraying across the street as the Big Wheel bounced once rather violently before he skidded sideways to a halt. One of his pennies bounced onto the grass beside the road, another lay face up in the sand next to the curb with the sun shining on Lincoln's imperfect nose.

The crowd of neighborhood first and second graders rushed over to him as Randall stood up, straddling his trusty steed.

"You did it!" came a cry from one of the boys in the crowd. "You passed the green chalk line!"

He beat Victor by two whole lines! Nobody had ever started such a run from the very top of the steep hill where they caught the bus to go to school every day.

Randall pushed his ski goggles up on top of his brother's hockey helmet and held his arms over his head, fingers signaling 'number one.' His peanut butter and jelly sandwich would taste even better today.

Having thus conquered "Bus Stop Hill" with the longest Big Wheel Jump of the spring, Randall took in the adulation and slaps on the back from his peers. Victor was busy picking up the loose change and planning the next jump of his own.

PHILADELPHIA, PENNSYLVANIA

Tyler held his father's hand as they walked down Archer Street in Philadelphia's "Little China Town." The cold wind made his chin numb. His green wool cap almost covered the five-year old's eyes.

His father, Hiroto, read a tourist map of the city, making sure they were on the right path to see the Liberty Bell. Liberty was an ironic word for Hiroto. He was first generation American, born to Japanese parents who had immigrated to the United States, settling in San Francisco in 1935. Hiroto was born two years later. When he was five, he and his family were forced by the United States government into the Manzanar Relocation Center. That was part of Executive Order 9066 which authorized the evacuation of all citizens of Japanese descent from the west coast. The attack on Pearl Harbor a few months earlier sent America to war and instantly created an anti-Japanese sentiment.

That world seemed so far away for Hiroto, but there were still many days when he wrestled with how this country, which he now loved, could cave to what he perceived as paranoia and suspend the rights of its citizens.

Now living on the east coast, it was important for Hiroto to show Tyler everything the country is and was. He broke tradition and married a Caucasian American, Jennifer. They were not married at a Shinto shrine, and Hiroto wondered if his parents would be disappointed in him if they had still been alive at the time. He told himself that because they considered themselves Americans, it was OK. Tyler was his pride and joy.

The steam coming up from the manholes in the street gave off a strange odor. Or maybe it was the man selling hot dogs from a cart. Crossing Hutcheson Avenue, Hiroto felt a tug on his arm from Tyler who had now stopped and was looking down the alley. A dirty looking man in a tattered olive Army jacket sat with his back against the wall, petting a small brown dog which looked more well-fed than the man himself. An Airborne patch was nearly torn off the jacket, which also had several tears in it.

"He looks hungry," the boy said innocently.

Hiroto squatted down beside his son, placing his arm around his shoulder. He could see his breath as he spoke.

"What do you want to do?" Hiroto asked.

"I want to give him something to eat, Daddy," Tyler said as he pulled the purple rubber coin case from his pocket. Pulling off his blue mittens, he thumbed a nickel and the worn penny with the scratched nose of the sixteenth president.

"OK," Hiroto sighed with a smile. "This will be your good deed for today."

He took the coins from his son, turned, and placed them in his pocket so his son could not see. He then pulled a dollar from his own wallet and bought two hot dogs from the man with the cart. The fat man in charge of the cart was arguing about football with a short younger man in a faded blue jacket and Philadelphia Eagles hat. Hiroto didn't know anything about whether the Dolphins or Jets were a better team and cared nothing for the NFL playoffs. It seemed important to the two men however, as neither deviated from their conversation during the whole transaction with Hiroto.

The man and the boy walked down the alley hand in hand. Hiroto gently pushed Tyler behind him as they came within five feet of the stranger.

Hiroto squatted and held the two hot dogs out. The dog twisted its head quizzically. The stranger looked up. His gray eyes seemed to be looking past him. Then he became lucid for a moment and reached for the hot dogs. He said nothing but nodded his head.

Hiroto nodded back, as Tyler peered from behind his father's legs. The stranger glanced at the boy briefly. He didn't quite register a smile, but the look still made Tyler's lips curl upward. The stranger broke off a piece of the hot dog to feed his pet, and then fed himself.

Father and son walked back to the main road. Tyler looked back to try to make eye contact with the stranger again, but the man was busy eating. The boy wondered why the man looked so sad. Why was he sitting out in the cold?

Hiroto felt sorry for the man. He wondered if the man was really an army veteran, perhaps from the war in Vietnam from the previous decade. He thought it was a shame that so many Americans did not treat the soldiers with honor. He respected American soldiers even though they acted as his warden early in his own life. His parents taught him all about honor, shame, and duty. They were conflicted when the Empire of Japan went to war with the United States. They wanted to be honorable, but they could not serve two masters honorably, in the traditional sense, at that time. The bombing of Pearl Harbor shamed them. Hiroto's father asked to serve in the U.S. Army, but because he was not a Nisei, or second generation American, he could not.

As they continued to their destination to see the Liberty Bell, Hiroto felt a sense of pride in the compassion his young son had shown. He held Tyler's hand once again with his right hand, while he kept his left hand warm in the pocket of his gray pants. Thumbing the change his son had given him to buy the hot dogs, Hiroto hoped his parents would be proud of him, and consider him as a man of honor, too.

WESTERN VIRGINIA

There was still fog on the mountain lake as Thad checked his rearview mirror and looked at his family. His infant son, T.J., was making some gurgling noises indicating that he was awake. His wife, Elexa, smiled as she held him in her lap.

"You OK?" she asked with a hopeful raised eyebrow. "First Christmas!"

Thad smiled as he pulled up to his parents' house and put the Jeep Cherokee in park.

"Yeah, first Christmas," Thad replied, trying to sound enthusiastic.

In his head, Thad knew he should have been excited. It was indeed T.J.'s first Christmas. There would be a lot of firsts this year. It was their first Christmas as a married couple, too, among other things. The "shotgun" marriage, as his father had called it, had been a sore spot with the old man. Marrying a Hispanic woman didn't sit well with his dad either. Thad remembered his father referring to Hispanics matter-of-factly as "wetbacks" and "beaners" as casually as anyone else would say "black" or "white." His father had a way of making conversations uncomfortable by saying little and looking away when he did speak.

Thad took a deep breath and allowed the cool air to wake him up and take full note of his senses as he grabbed the backpack and suitcase out of the back. Elexa grabbed T.J. and they headed up the stairs for the front door.

Peeking in the glass beside the door, Thad saw his mom on a ladder trying to hang Christmas decorations, so he didn't bother to ring the bell and walked in.

The sound of Barbara Streisand singing Christmas tunes blared throughout the house.

"You're here!" his mother, Peggy, squealed.

In her early seventies, Peggy could have passed for mid-fifties. She was agile and sharp. Knowing his mother, Thad didn't blink with her quick descent down the ladder and bouncing toward the couple.

The older woman hugged her son and her daughter-in-law before giving her full attention to the child, gleefully lifting him from Elexa's arms.

Peggy spun around and began her baby-talk with T.J., while Elexa resisted the urge to say, "be careful." As it was her first child, Elexa had to constantly remind herself that T.J. wasn't made of glass and to relax more.

Still, it wasn't always easy.

"Come. Sit," Peggy ordered as she plopped herself down on the couch beside the half-decorated Christmas tree.

Thad walked over to the stereo and turned Streisand down so it would be easier to talk. He also hated that damn album, but Mom insisted on playing it every year while she decorated and when they opened presents.

The two women fawned over T.J. and after answering a few obligatory questions about work and if they're getting enough sleep, Thad made his way to the kitchen. The gumball machine was filled to the top.

"Dad could never resist the sweets," Thad thought to himself as he picked up a penny from the bowl on top of the gumball machine. Staring at Mr. Lincoln's imperfect face, he replaced the penny in the bowl and smiled. "There's another thing Dad can't resist."

He opened the fridge and smiled as he saw the cold six pack of beer waiting. Mom always had a stocked fridge. Dad always enjoys a cold beer in the morning, between breakfast and lunch. Just one.

Looking out the back window, he saw the smoke rising up from the fire pit in the yard. He grabbed a pair of beers and decided it was time to talk to Dad.

Thad was thirty now, but even as an adult, he always felt like a child when speaking to his father. Maybe it's because of his dad's manner. He never spoke first and never spoke unless he had something to say. The tension of the last year made it tougher.

"I'll be out back," Thad called out as Elexa and Peggy continued their conversation.

The backyard was his dad's sanctuary. You could see the sun rise and set pretty well from there. The view of the water was great, too. The old man loved to come out there and chop wood, read a book, or just stare for hours at the splendor of this little piece of uncomplicated world.

There were two chairs next to the fire pit. Thad took a drag of his beer and placed the other on the arm of his dad's favorite chair while starting the conversation.

"First Christmas," Thad said weakly. "Mom has things looking great inside. She always knows how to make it feel like a holiday. I'm sure she even lit this fire for you."

Thad wasn't happy with his own small talk, so he pressed on.

"Look, this last year has been really tough for me. I know you weren't happy about, well about us having a baby and having to get married, but Elexa is my wife, and she's a great girl."

Thad took another swig of his beer in silence, somewhat disappointed in the one-sided conversation. He loved his dad, but he sure could make things complicated.

"She's a great cook, too," he continued and then pointed at his father, expecting an interruption. "And, no, she doesn't cook tacos and burritos every night. And you know what? She likes baseball! I mean, she's not a Yankees fan, but..."

Thad's voice trailed off. He thought he was lightening the mood, but now the silence was just awkward. He took another long pull of his beer and placed the empty bottle on the arm of the other chair.

"Honey, is it OK if we come out?" Elexa called from the back door.

Thad waived her over as he swallowed the last of his beer.

The proud young father cradled his baby in his left arm, and with his right hand, he deftly popped the top off the beer still resting on his dad's chair and grabbed the top of the long-neck.

"Dad, meet T.J., your grandson," Thad said proudly. "I know you're thinking it's 'Thad, Jr.,' but it's not. It's 'Thad' after me and 'Joseph' after you. I hope you will love him as I do."

He placed T.J. on the small flat grave marker between the two chairs.

"T.J., this is your grandad. This was his favorite spot, and this is where he wanted to be buried. I hope you'll love it here, too."

Thad took a long pull of his dad's beer and thought out loud, "First Christmas without him."

DOTHAN, ALABAMA

The deacon stood behind the priest as the funeral began. Although they were roughly the same age, the deacon appeared younger. He was pleasantly surprised at the turnout for the funeral, but also a little concerned as there weren't enough seats for everyone.

Many of the mourners lined the back of church and curled up the side aisles outside the pews. Tom was a popular guy. The gray casket was in front of the first row, before the steps leading to the altar.

The old priest didn't seem to notice the discomfort of the crowd as he stared into his scriptures and read at a painfully slow pace.

While he wanted to listen to the words of the priest, the deacon's eyes kept searching those of the family in the front row. He had known them all well and for a long time.

Judy, the widow was holding up pretty well. Her eyes were moist, but she was holding back the tears. The deacon thought she looked lovely, but tired, in her black dress. He was able to see past the lines in her face, remembering a younger version of the beautiful woman.

Behind her, Tom's best friend, Larry, shifted his weight uncomfortably from his right leg to his left. He was uncomfortable, but not impatient. He could tell that he was saddened by the loss of his longtime friend.

An older man having a brief coughing fit across the aisle gained the deacon's attention now. "He's probably thinking about how many people will show up when it's his turn to die," the deacon thought. "There's nothing like getting older to gain a heightened sense of your own mortality."

Next to him was the kid from the bank that used to date one of Tom's daughters. A younger man in his early thirties. "Nice kid," the deacon thought. "But you can tell he doesn't want to be here. He's probably thinking about where he's going to go out tonight. He would have been happier if he had stayed with Caroline."

The priest began his homily and the congregation wedged in their seats. Some fanned themselves with the sheets of paper that had the lyrics to the hymns. Others took their sport coats off and laid them across their legs as the priest droned on.

Once again, the deacon tried to stay engaged with what the old priest was saying, but his attention was constantly being called elsewhere. Again, he found the family in the front row. He was fascinated by their faces. He had been to many funerals before, but this one was more personal.

"Oh, Darlene," he thought as he noticed the oldest daughter weeping. She was in her forties now and always looked a few years older. "She never had much luck in life, but she's done OK."

The deacon shook his head, remembering Darlene's problems with alcohol and the child she had out of wedlock. She overcame her addictions, however, and she put herself through school while raising the boy, Michael, on her own. He wasn't judging her, just remembering the struggles the family had with getting her on the right path.

The old priest must have said something witty because there was a chuckle from below, and the deacon was embarrassed that he wasn't paying attention and couldn't share in enjoying the laugh.

Even Tom's younger daughter, Ella, was smiling for a moment, as she rubbed her mother's back. The deacon was more upset now that he missed the joke, but it's not like he could ask the priest to say it again.

"Ah, Ella," the deacon thought. "She grew up so fast. I still remember the time she ran up to the altar right in the middle of a service when she was a toddler."

The deacon let out a soft laugh at the memory, as she had also pulled her dress over her head that day in front of the congregation, which mortified her mother. The deacon collected himself and realized nobody had heard his chortle.

The congregation stood as the homily was now over. The deacon proudly chanted Psalm 23 from memory with those in attendance, but his eyes were still locked on the front pew.

Tom's youngest grandson, Byron, was fidgeting in the pew next to Ella. He was only four years old. He wiggled his shoulders back and forth. Everyone said he resembled Tom.

The deacon smiled as he watched the boy fidget with a penny he had pulled from his pocket. His grandfather would always give him pennies to buy some gum when they went to the corner store together. Byron went to put the penny back, but he missed his pocket and it rolled out into the center aisle. The boy looked left and right but didn't see it. He looked up toward the altar, and the deacon tried to move his eyes to the right, hoping the boy would get the hint to look in that direction. Deep down, he knew he wouldn't.

Just then, the sun broke through the clouds outside and shone through the stained-glass window, projecting light directly into the center aisle and lighting up the face of the old, chipped penny.

"Ye of little faith," the deacon admonished himself and then smiled.

Byron seemed to take the cue and spotted the coin. He briefly broke the grasp of his mother's hand and retrieved his prize, much to the delight of many in the first several rows.

The deacon knew it was hot in the church, but there was a part of him that didn't want the service to end. He looked back at Judy, now a widow. She was crying for the first time.

He wanted to wipe her tears, but he knew he couldn't do that.

The deacon did not wish to be emotional, so he switched his gaze toward the top of the church. He had never really paid attention to the interior construction, but it was quite marvelous with stone and wooden beams holding together this small but still magnificent structure.

"How did I miss this?" the deacon asked himself as the priest continued with a prayer.

Before he knew it, the final hymn was being sung. The deacon was now sorry he had missed everything that had been said. He was mesmerized by the sadness in some and joy in others. Not joy that Tom was dead, but joy in the stories that must have been told during the homily. In some ways, it was perfect.

The congregation slowly moved from the pews when the hymn ended. Family members hugged each other again and wiped their tears away. Their faces registered a look of finality.

"This is it, I guess," the deacon thought.

The priest ambled down to the front pew to shake the hands of the family members. They all focused their gaze on the old man, except for Byron. The youngster looked over the top of the casket, as if staring into the eyes of the deacon, and waved.

The deacon smiled and waved back. He wanted to go down and hug the boy one last time, but he knew he couldn't do that. It was time for Deacon Tom to return home.

WILMINGTON, NC

Professor Owen Jaffe stared straight up at the ceiling as he leaned back in the wheeled wooden chair. His feet rested comfortably atop the desk in his classroom. This was the best day of each semester.

As the red hand on the second clock across from his desk completed another full circle and indicated it was now 9:05 a.m., he was ready to start his final exam. He picked a crumb from his morning muffin that had stuck onto his old beige sweater and popped it into his mouth.

"So, you're the only brave souls to take me up on my offer," Jaffe said as he rose from his desk and addressed the three students seated randomly in his fifteen-seat classroom.

The three students, two males and one female looked at each other for a moment, all with confident grins. Professor Jaffe had published a few novels, none of them making any best seller lists, but they were all well-reviewed. Now in his late fifties, he continued to teach to make additional income that his novels did not provide. His brown hair was now thin on top, but his brown and gray speckled beard and mustache were well-groomed.

"As you know, I only allow fifteen students into my fiction writing class each semester," Jaffe continued. "All you had to do to pass my class is turn in the two short stories I asked you to write during the semester and read them aloud to the class on your assigned day to allow for critique."

Professor Jaffe sat down on top of one of the desks in the front row, resting his old brown leather shoes on the seat of the chair as he continued.

"As long as I didn't think you mailed it in, everyone in the class would get anywhere from a 'C+' to a 'B+' as a grade. The only way to get an 'A' and to earn my recommendation for a post graduate position is to take my optional final exam. Looks like you three are the only brave souls this semester."

Hopping from the desk, he eyed his three students. He always thought of his students as possible characters in his next book. He absorbed them one-by-one.

In the middle was Dana Brice. The young lady with the perfect face that probably looked great without an ounce of makeup. A loose white sweater and blue jeans flattered her. It was her voice that always intrigued Professor Jaffe. It was somewhat deeper than most of the girls with only the slightest southern accent. Professor Jaffe often found himself staring a little too long at her beautiful green eyes and long brown hair. He wasn't the only one.

David Cook was the cocky kid to his right. Donning casual khaki pants and an untucked polo shirt, the fraternity boy also liked to attend class carrying a "to go" cup. Professor Jaffe never called him out on it, but he knew it was gin and tonic more often than not, as opposed to a simple Sprite. He would allow David to enjoy his coolness.

Malcolm Moore was off to the left. The only black student in the class, he stood out not because of the color of his skin but for the richness and different perspective he brought to his stories. At over six feet tall with a lean but muscular physique, Professor Jaffe assumed he was a pretty good athlete, but never asked if he was a member of any of the UNC Wilmington athletics teams. He always dressed well, and today was no exception.

The professor stuffed his right hand into his front pants pocket and fished out a penny, holding it up to the right of his head. Nothing remarkable to see, other than the imperfection on President Lincoln's nose.

"No writing today," Jaffe said. "Just tell me a story."

He paused to look each in the eye. "It's simple. Let's pretend for a moment you all believe in God. Today, God is going to appear to you and tell you He is going to give you the power to do anything you want without any repercussions to you on how you use it. You can even decide how long He will give you this power. Give me the outline of your idea and then narrate any detailed part of your story."

The professor stood there for a moment, making eye contact with each of his students. "You've got fifteen minutes to scribble some notes down, then we'll start." He looked at his watch and said, "Go."

Jaffe returned to his desk, pleased with how clever he was and waited.

"Alright, Cook, you're up first," Jaffe said, flipping the penny to David after fifteen minutes expired. "A penny for your thoughts. Amaze me."

Catching the penny, David smacked it face down confidently on the desk and straightened his posture.

"Alright," David began. "The back story begins with Benjamin. Small middle school kid who was always getting picked on. After one particular day of getting pushed around, he hits his head on a locker and nearly passes out. Still a bit woozy, he feels a hand on his shoulder, and a gentle, white-haired man, who appears to have a glow about him, asks him if he is okay. Benjamin tells the guy what happened and how he feels useless and can't do anything right and how he wishes he could just have one day where everything worked out. The man still appears to be glowing and with the hall suddenly quiet and void of any other students, Benjamin gasps in the presence of the Almighty."

David paused and looked at his classmates who were mildly hooked on his introduction, then continued.

"The old guy places his hands on Benjamin's head and says, 'I promise you, if you believe it, you can do it.' So now Benjamin is suddenly filled with an air of confidence and as the man helps him up, the bell rings and students spill into the hall from all of the classrooms. One of the bullies appears and shoulders Benjamin into the locker. The anger builds up quickly inside, and instead of just collapsing and giving up like he always had done, he hears it again, 'if you believe it, you can do it.' Out of nowhere, Benjamin thrusts the heel of his hand up from his hip to the chin of the bully, knocking him to the floor and rendering him silly. He looks for his glowing friend, but the man is nowhere to be seen, so at this point Benjamin gets the feeling of divine intervention at play."

Jaffe merely raised one eyebrow as David made eye contact with him.

"So now he's quickly becoming confident in everything he does," David licked his lips as he continued his story. "Benjamin continues to overcome obstacles throughout the day that had normally challenged him. He wins the class spelling bee after normally getting knocked out in the first round. He perfectly assembles a motor in shop class after never getting more than two or three nuts together. He even hits all four shots he takes in the basketball game at gym class after not making a shot all year. So, you get the idea. His confidence is growing, and this is going on all day. At the end of the day, he figures he would really impress the world around him. He climbs the stairs to the roof of the three-story school building. A crowd assembles as he stands perched on the ledge looking down. Children are pointing up at him. A teacher is screaming at him to get down. Another teacher is running inside, scaling the staircase two steps at a time to try to reach Benjamin."

David doesn't hesitate, but he can feel his classmates leaning in a little bit, as if they can't wait to hear what happens next.

"Maybe it's to impress a girl. Maybe he wants to be Superman. 'If you believe it, you can do it,' he says again. Benjamin prepares to dive out from the ledge and at the same time sees the horrified look of the gentle, white-haired man below. There is no confidence or pleasure in the man's face. The man he thought was God was merely a janitor. He taught Benjamin that if he really did believe it, he really could do almost anything if he at least tried. It was all inside him, and he really could do anything … well, almost anyway."

"That's horrible!" Dana mistakenly said out loud.

"Horrible because Benjamin dies or horrible because you don't like the story?" Jaffe asked rhetorically.

"Hey, that's off the top of my head," David said, defensively. "If I have more time to think about it, I might have one of the bullies actually make it up to the roof and grab his shirt tail or something. Or maybe I'll go total science-fiction and have the kid actually fly. Kind of Peter Pan-like."

"Yeah, and after reading that, you'll have kids jumping off buildings screaming 'If you believe it, you can do it,'" Malcolm said while shaking his head.

"Alright, alright," Jaffe interrupted.

The professor picked up the penny from David's desk.

"What have you got Malcolm?" Jaffe said as he flipped the coin to the student. "A penny for your thoughts. Amaze me."

Jaffe turned and sat back down atop of the desk, elbow on his knee, resting his chin on his hand.

"There's an orphanage," Malcolm said, reading from his hastily scribbled notes. "There's a boy, we'll call him Michael. Michael is six and hoping to get adopted. Sadly, Michael had lost his parents in a car accident when he was a baby and lived with his uncle. He was taken away from his uncle when they found out the guy was touching him, you know, inappropriately."

Malcolm had their attention.

"So, he prayed to God every night to make him stronger. To make him a big brave knight, like in his story books. To give him parents who loved him. In a dream, he's told by a being, we won't call him God per-say, that his wish will be granted, but somewhat conditionally. He eventually finds himself living two lives simultaneously, or so he thinks. He's living as a warrior, slaying dragons, rescuing maidens, and conquering kingdoms. He's also living as a little boy in the orphanage. Each version of himself is aware of the other's successes, failures and struggles and he is tormented by trying to bridge those emotions together. It seems that for every good thing that happens in one life, something bad happens in another. I haven't worked all that out yet. As this goes on after a few months or maybe a year, he realizes that the only way to find happiness was for there to be only one 'him,' and that this gift that was given to him by the deity, was more like a trap and is perhaps evil. So, he is tormented as the adult version of himself feels the pain of loss in battle along with the joy of his conquests, and the boy in the orphanage can't shake the pain of his past. He no longer wishes to be disappointed by not having parents and stays in his room while the other kids play. More and more the two personalities are aware of the other, and the pressure of one of them having to sacrifice himself for the sake of the other is growing. The older Michael wants the younger version to have a long happy life, but the younger

Michael can't get past his own pain and won't leave his room. He's so ashamed."

Jaffe and Dana made eye contact, each seeming to understand the root of the fable. Malcolm's voice seemed to tremble just a little bit. He closed his eyes as he finished painting a picture with his words to describe the ultimate victor in his story. It was as if he had already written this part of the story as it progressed from summary to poetry.

"The blue sky offered no solace to his shame," Malcolm said. "The man walked through his village with the old shield dragging at his feet. The opponents he had slain were uncounted, but he was by no means undefeated. The monsters he faced in the world were no match for those that hid under his bed as a child. Exhausted, he lay on the bed with all his armor gone, save the lone ring of gold on his finger. It was all he would need, and it was everything to lose. Elsewhere in time, the child put his toys away and opened the bedroom door at last."

Silence in the classroom. A tear ran down Dana's cheek.

Malcolm slowly opened his eyes, realizing for the first time that they had been closed. He made eye-contact with Professor Jaffe, who still had his chin resting on his hand, but his lips curled slightly upward in a knowing, seemingly affirming grin.

"Nicely done," Jaffe said as the other students sat quietly, still taking in Malcolm's tale.

Jaffe hopped off the desk and palmed the penny from in front of Malcolm, spun on his heel and bowed slightly in front of Dana.

"Alright Ms. Brice," Jaffe said as he flipped her the coin. "A penny for your thoughts. Amaze me."

Dana caught the coin in her left hand without breaking eye contact with the professor. He slowly backed away to the desk in the front row, assuming his usual position. Once again, he scanned the eyes of his students, momentarily trying to guess what was going through their minds.

"Caroline had always been a woman of faith," Dana began. "Raised in the Baptist Church, she was one of the few children who loved Sunday school. She had many questions about her faith, but the questions were only so she could make her faith stronger and share the good news with others. God had tested her faith at different times in her life, but it did not falter. As she became an adult, she had visions of angels when she slept. On her fortieth birthday, she awoke with painful sores on her wrists and feet – signs of the stigmata."

David yawned audibly. His eyes repeatedly moving from Dana's eyes to the loose v-neck area of her sweater, hoping to see more cleavage. Dana didn't notice, or at least pretended as such.

"When she is fifty," Dana continued, "An angel appears to her and says that God wants to reward her for her faith and will give her the power of one miracle per day for a month to do whatever will make her happy. Caroline wonders if this is another test. She thinks 'Surely God would not give me this power if it wasn't meant to serve Him and help His people. But is it wrong for me to presume to know what is most important to God? If I do something that was not meant to be, then would this butterfly-effect cause great harm? Then again, God is omniscient, so He already knows what I will do.' This cyclical thinking becomes somewhat maddening for Caroline, and three days have gone by before she finally realizes she has not done anything.

"The power for good has become somewhat terrifying for her, and she decides to start small. She is taking the purse with the donations for the homeless shelter to the bank. Knowing it is a small sum, she places her hands on the purse and prays before going up to the teller. What should have been a few hundred dollars, is now more than $200,000. Enough to run the floundering shelter for more than a year and cover all that was on its wish-list. There's no telling who is more surprised, Caroline or the teller. At this point Caroline is sad because she realized for the very first time, she had doubted her faith. 'Never again,' she swears."

Dana looks back down at her notes before continuing. Malcolm seems to be doodling. David is still ogling.

"As the days go by, she sees the homeless find themselves, and those that were poor are now finding success – richness in their lives in finding self-worth. There is a beautiful story each day, and each day she tries to think bigger and how her one miracle per day can be spread to help more people. Not once has she done anything for herself, however. She frequents the children's hospital and cures those that were incurable. On the fifteenth day, she is driving a friend. It's around 7 p.m., but it's not dark, because it's late in the spring."

Dana turned to look at David who was unaware because he was still trying to peek down her sweater.

"Her friend, a younger woman who is pregnant, is riding in the back seat with her two-year-old daughter," Dana continued. "She glances at the toddler in her rearview mirror, not seeing the drunken fraternity boy who had just left happy hour and had crossed the center lane coming in the opposite direction."

Dana's voice goes from soft and slow, to louder and with an excited pace.

"There is a terrible crash! A fast crunching of steel and the shattering of glass. Then all is quiet. Her car rests on its side. She is bleeding out and knows she has a few moments of consciousness. The pregnant friend and the baby are bloodied. She does not hear a sound from the other vehicle driven by the young man. She clasps her hands together as if to say her one prayer. But who to save? Is she the Good Samaritan who saves the other driver? What about the pregnant woman and her unborn baby? Could this unborn child be the next savior? Should she save herself, for self-preservation reasons? Or should she save herself because she still has fifteen days of miracles where she can save many more people?

"The sound of an ambulance siren is heard in the distance, and the last words spoken in the scene are 'Thy will be done. Amen.' Then there is nothing."

The room was silent for a moment.

"That's it?" David asked. Apparently, he had been listening. "What's the conclusion? You can't leave it like that."

"Yours wasn't finished either," Dana replied, eyes turned to David but her face still pointing to the front of the class.

Professor Jaffe held out his arms, bringing the attention of the three students back to him.

"Good stuff," Jaffe said. "Really. Lots of possibilities with these ideas. I'd encourage you to pursue these and let them play out and bring them back to me if you want."

"So, who wins?" David interrupted.

Before Jaffe could answer, the door to the classroom noisily opened and clanged against the side wall. Russ Blackmon's entrance wasn't graceful, but it fit his appearance. He looked like he had just woken up wearing the clothes from the night before. Probably the same clothes he wore to rugby practice. They were covered in dirt and grass stains, and there was dried blood on his left knee. His brown hair was all over the place, and he reeked of cheap draft beer and cigarette smoke from the bar. And was that a bruise or a hickey on his neck?

This wasn't the first time Russ had made such an appearance in class, but he was usually at least on time. He hadn't bothered to set his alarm. His stories were normally entertaining, but not great. Still, Professor Jaffe somewhat admired the fly-by-the-seat-of-his-pants quality of Russ. He had a keen ability to produce extemporaneously, and a personality that didn't rub anyone the wrong way. Although there were times that his penchant for not showering and arriving in class smelling like rugby and the bar made his classmates wish he would sit on the other side of the room.

"This should be good," Jaffe thought to himself as he smiled without realizing it.

Jaffe looked at the clock on the wall.

"Still fifteen minutes left in our exam period," the professor said and explained the rules again. He flipped the wild boy his coin. "A penny for your thoughts. Amaze me."

MILWAUKEE, WISCONSIN

"What are you doing?" Chris asked Kendall as he caught up with her on the sidewalk, brushing his sandy brown hair out of his eyes with his hand, while adjusting his backpack. "I wanted to borrow your notes from psych class."

Kendall hesitated and then responded without taking her eyes off the homeless man across the street. A cool breeze blew her dark hair in front of her face. "Have you seen that guy? He's … fascinating."

The homeless man was in layers of shabby clothing. Patchy facial hair adorned his chin and parts of his cheeks and upper lip. He seemed to be arguing with himself as he paced and gestured with his arms.

"Tommy Two-Times? He's around here all the time," Chris chuckled.

"Why do you call him that?

"My roommate, Ryan, noticed him one day and tried to talk to him," Chris explained. "He was pretty incoherent and just started blathering on about being in the here and now and also being in the 1940s, or something like that. So, we called him 'Tommy Two-Times.'"

Kendall could not take her eyes off the man. She was always the caring soul who wanted to solve everyone's problems.

"C'mon. Let's go grab some lunch before class," Chris pleaded.

"Hold on," Kendall said as she drifted off the sidewalk to cross the street and get a closer look at the man.

"What are you doing? You don't want to get near him, Kendall. He's crazy. C'mon, let's go."

Kendall casually waved him off, flicking her wrist behind her as she crossed the street.

"Tommy" didn't see her as he continued his pacing for a moment and finally sat down on the bench at the bus stop. His head was down as he continued to mumble.

Kendall approached and casually sat down on the other end of the bench, while Chris shuffled across the street, somewhat alarmed that his friend got so close to the man. The layers of clothing he wore made Kendall uncomfortable for him.

"Hey," Kendall said to the man softly. "Are you OK?"

The man known only as Tommy kept his head down, but his mumbling, shaking, and gesturing suddenly stopped. "Do you see it? Is it really here, in this time?"

"Do I see what?"

He pointed to sidewalk where a dirty penny lay, face up.

"That. Do you see that coin? Tell me, can you see it?" he asked, drawing out each word slowly.

Kendall followed his finger, slid forward on the bench, and peered down at the coin. "Yes sir. Do you want it?" she asked as she scooped up the coin. "It's an old one. It's scratched up a little bit on the front."

The man exhaled in relief. "OK. That's in the now. That's good. That's good," he said excitedly.

"Do you want it?" she asked.

The man didn't respond directly, but instead looked away, to his right. "It all looks right." Then he turned to face Kendall for the first time. "Do you know what year it is?"

Kendall was taken aback in seeing the man's face for the first time. Both of his eyes were clouded over. His stringy peppered hair hung from his forehead. She smiled kindly as she thought the man was clearly mentally ill.

"It's 1990. Are you OK? Do you need to go somewhere?"

He stared back down at his feet. "No. No. I'm where I'm supposed to be. And….." he paused as if he lost his train of thought. "I'm when I'm supposed to be."

The man relaxed for a moment.

Chris walked slowly toward the bench but opted not to sit down. He was trying to be sly to get Kendall to leave, waving his hand at his hip, craning his neck, and mouthing, "C'mon."

Kendall waved him off again.

"What do you mean, 'when you're supposed to be?'" she pressed on. "Are you late for something?"

"I'm here now, but sometimes, I'm there, then. Now is now, but sometimes now is then," the man said as his agitation rose again, and his speech quickened. "I look and I see things that are here now, but sometimes I see things that were here that aren't here now. They were here then, but they're not here now, but I'm here now and I'm there then, at least I'm there at part of then."

Kendall shook her head trying to make sense of his rambling. "I don't understand. Do you think you're in a different time?"

The man thrust his arms straight down and stood up quickly with his head still pointed down at the pavement, his frustration was growing.

"I don't know when I belong," he said. "I look down this street, and sometimes things are like they were before you were here! The buildings are different. The cars. The people. They're then, but they're not now, but I see them now even though they're in the then and can still see some of the now!"

Chris rolled his eyes and then made eye contact with Kendall, mouthing "Tommy Two-Times" while swirling his index finger by his head to indicate what he thought of the man's mental status.

The man sat back down, out of breath. Kendall thought he was beginning to cry. She reached her arm out to touch him on the shoulder. A comforting gesture.

"Don't touch me," the man said as he pulled away. "I don't want you to get trapped with me; bouncing between the now and the then."

Kendall recoiled. "OK. I'm sorry. I'm just trying to understand. Can I get you something?"

"I'm thirsty," he said.

It was Kendall's turn to mouth something silently to Chris. "Go across the street and get him a soda or something." She handed him a random bunch of change from her purse, including the old penny.

Chris' jaw dropped but realized he wasn't winning this battle, so he impatiently spun on his heel and jaywalked across the street to the convenience store.

"So, you think you are living in two times at once?" Kendall surmised, trying to see if anything from her psych class would translate. "You're seeing things from the past?"

The man rubbed his temples and spoke lucidly for the first time. "I see what is here today. Sometimes it is overlapped by the past. I see people that aren't here today, but nobody else sees them and I don't know why. I see the now and the then. The people in the now, don't see the then, and the people in the then don't see the now." His cloudy eyes seemed to plead with Kendall as he faced her again, hoping she would understand.

"When is the then?" she asked, sounding like she was grasping his concept.

"Sometime during the war. The big one. 1940-something," he said.

"Like the coin?"

"Like the coin." The man was starting to relax again. "I need to stay in the now. I don't want to go back to the then."

Chris returned with the soda and stuck it in front of the man's face as an offering. He took it without a word. Not even a thank you.

The man popped the top on the can and took a long pull of the sweet, bubbly drink. After exhaling with relief, he let out a loud belch. Chris and Kendall laughed.

Her curiosity satisfied; Kendall decided it was time to go. She stood and tugged on her purse as a silent gesture for Chris to give the man the spare change.

Chris took the hint, and extended his palm with a couple of quarters, a nickel, and the old, scratched penny. "Here. Maybe you can get yourself another drink later or something."

The man raised his head with a brief smile. His expression changed quickly as he stared across the street as if he had seen a ghost. "It's not there! Do you see it? That old truck, too." Glancing down at Chris' hand, he only saw the 1943 penny. "No!" he screamed as he slapped the hand away, the coins scattering on the sidewalk.

"What's wrong?" Kendall shrieked. "I don't see a truck or anything but the store. Wait!"

The man turned and began to run in the opposite direction. "I can't go to the then!"

Kendall and Chris stood in stunned silence as the man continued to scream and run away.

Behind them, the old penny rolled on its edge to the corner, coming to rest at the foot of an elderly man in a gray suit and fedora who was humming.

"Must be my lucky day," the man said as he snatched the coin and resumed his tune. "Hey there, is that the Chattanooga Choo-Choo."

PRESCOTT, ARIZONA

"Are you done with your tea yet?" Harvey asked. He was seated on the couch but was leaning forward in anticipation of getting up.

June, his wife, had actually finished her cup, but wanted to sit just a minute longer. "Not yet, Dear."

June was tired. She had been tired a lot lately. At seventy-five, she had aged pretty well. Her hair still had a little bit of color in it. Well, it was more of a dark gray mixed in with white hair.

Harvey loved his morning walk. Diabetes had taken most of his sight a few years back, and although he shook quite a bit and walked awkwardly, he loved his morning walk. He was two years her senior, but he looked older. There were just thin patches of white hair on the sides of his head, leading to a little trail of white in the back. A few random strands stuck up around the top. The only colors there were the brown liver spots.

Harvey's eyes were cloudy. Dressed in a white t-shirt and khaki shorts, he was a site in his blue socks that rode halfway up his shins. He liked his new blue sneakers, even if he didn't know they were blue. They gave him "extra pep in his step." At least that's what he told June every day.

June looked lovingly at Harvey and felt guilty for wanting to sit longer. They had actually walked an hour ago, but Harvey's "senior moments" were becoming more frequent, and he forgot. At least he still had a lot of energy, she thought.

Placing her cup down so Harvey could hear it, she smiled. "Let's go."

Harvey grimaced as he got up without help and felt his way to the front door. Although he couldn't see much of anything, he thought he was more independent than he really was. He looked so feeble and helpless when he walked, not just because he was blind. His muscles were suffering atrophy, so he staggered more than anything. There was also the cruel paradox that he couldn't remember that he was often forgetful.

June hooked her arm around his and led him outside. It was a pleasant morning. Dry, but not too hot to walk. Not yet anyway.

They took a left at the end of the walkway. Harvey shuffled behind June. His mouth always half agape. June didn't know if he was aware that his mouth always sagged open, but she didn't want him to feel badly about it.

The couple made their way slowly down the same road. Harvey took pride in pointing out that he knew where they were at different times on their walk.

"That's McHenry's house, right?" Harvey asked, confident he was in the right spot.

"Yep, pretty close," June said, even though they were still about thirty yards from that house. She didn't want him to be discouraged. She had suggested a while back that he count his steps to various landmarks, that way he would always know where he was.

Harvey used to talk a lot on their walks. He would always tell her he loved her. Nowadays, it was hit or miss. Sometimes he said nothing at all. He just stared with his sightless eyes, mouth open, as if he didn't know who or where he was. Some days, he was more lucid and liked to talk about how he remembered the neighborhood when he could see.

June never corrected him. It was sad that he was wrong more often than he was right, but she didn't have the heart to tell him. She didn't like to think about the day that would come when he couldn't remember who she was.

A car tooted its horn as it passed the elderly couple. June waved, not paying attention to who it was.

"Was that Jenny?" Harvey asked.

June didn't know a Jenny but obliged. "Yes, I think it was."

There was a part of June that thought about getting help to take care of Harvey, but she didn't know where to start. The couple's only daughter, Olivia, lived in Toronto. Although she called often, she didn't visit much. Olivia was really into her career.

When Harvey was quiet, she would daydream about the good memories of their lives together. He always doted on her. He was corny but tried to be romantic and sweet. For years he would write her little notes every day. Other than cooking the meals, he wouldn't let her do any work around the house.

Now, she had to do everything. Soon after losing his vision, he had been slipping away, mentally, and it broke her heart. What else could she do but take care of this sweet man who had taken care of her for so long?

June spotted the little Swanson girl behind a homemade lemonade stand. Because it was her second walk of the day, June could use a beverage, and Harvey probably did as well, even if he didn't know he did.

"Harvey," June said. "Do you have any change? Little Darby Swanson is selling lemonade."

Harvey reflexively fished around in his pockets. "Here," he said, handing his bride an old penny, a nickel, and a loose button. "Get two if you want."

June sighed. While she wanted to keep giving Harvey chances to take care of her, she knew she was in charge and was always prepared. Pulling, two quarters out of her own pocket, she placed them in the can to pay, while dropping the other items, minus the button, in the jar labeled "tips." The nickel and the worn and chipped penny clinked as they were the first of the day. Lincoln and Jefferson faced each other.

June lovingly placed the cup in Harvey's hand so he could drink. He dribbled a little on his chin, but he didn't seem to mind. She drank hers quicker than she thought she would and made a show of exhaling to let Darby know how much she enjoyed it.

June and the little girl exchanged a "thank you" and the old couple continued their slow walk.

The road circled back towards their house, and they were well beyond the halfway point when Harvey spoke up. "Are we almost home, Dear? I'm kind of tired today for some reason."

"Yes, Dear. Just a few more blocks," June said.

The sun had mercifully stayed behind the clouds for most of their walk, otherwise it might have been more difficult. June didn't mind that they were making their second walk. She really had nothing else to do today, nor almost any day.

She thought about Thursday. That's when she went to the grocery store. That was the hard day because she no longer felt like she could leave Harvey alone at the house. He could fall or bump his head, or he might have one of his moments and forget where he was. She could just picture him calling out and not remembering where she had gone, and she didn't want to put him through that.

Taking him to the store wasn't much easier, although it gave him some more exercise. When he was lucid, it was fun because he would stop in the cereal aisle and beg her to get something unhealthy, like Cap'n Crunch. Or when he'd get a whiff from the bakery, he'd want to buy something sweet, like cakes or pies. She always did. What could it hurt at this point? Sadly, he would forget about those treasures when they got home, which wasn't the worse thing in the world since she didn't allow him to eat much of it due to his diabetes.

That was Thursday's problem.

For now, it was time to get him home.

They made their way to the front of the house, and Harvey found himself again.

"We're home, aren't we?"

June thought how he actually sounded like himself.

"Yes, Dear. Are you ready to relax or do you want to take a bath?" She asked.

"I may just lie down for a spell until lunchtime."

"That will be fine, Dear," June said as she ushered him in the front door. He let go of her hand and felt his way to the couch and rested.

June went into the kitchen and made herself a glass of water. She sat on a barstool, not wanting to look at the letter she had opened yesterday. She left it out in the open, but she wasn't worried about Harvey being able to read it.

As she sipped her water, June thought about the cancer that was running rampant through her body and the confirmation that there were no other options. She was often in pain but didn't show it.

She stared at her husband on the couch and felt guilty. Not for anything she had done, but for her hope that Harvey would go first and go soon, so that he wouldn't be alone when she was gone.

"June," Harvey said, raising his head from the couch. "Do you mind if we skip our walk today? I'm tired for some reason."

"That's fine, Dear," June said. "I'm tired, too."

FEBRUARY 1995

NEAR COLUMBUS, GEORGIA

The bus rolled past the Suwanee Swifty on Highway 41. The rain continued to fall outside as the lamps of the twenty-year-old Blue Bird showed only the two yellow lines in the middle of the road. From his usual window seat four rows back on the left side, Jay barely felt the cold water as it splashed in the pane of the sliding window. The window had always leaked when it rained, but this was his seat on every trip. Whether it was Jacksonville, Fla., Columbus, Ga., Pembroke, N.C., or anywhere in between, this was his seat.

Most of the basketball players donned headsets listening to their Discman. Jay didn't have one. His stare usually alternated between the passing sights outside the window to his left, ranging from long abandoned shacks overgrown by trees on old country state highways to the headlights of oncoming traffic on the interstates in the bigger cities.

When he wasn't gazing out the window, he stared straight ahead. David, the assistant coach, always sat in front of him. The neat and short cropped hair of the assistant coach had a peppered look to it even though, like Jay, he was only in his late twenties. The backwards z-shaped scar in the back of his head always made Jay wonder how it got there, but he never asked.

Seeing the lights of the interstate approaching Jay knew they would stop at the McDonald's/Exxon near the entrance.

The team had already had its postgame pizza which was waiting for them on the bus after the game. It never tasted good after a loss. Still, everyone knew the players would eat again anywhere they stopped. Jay always saved half of his sack lunch the Central State University cafeteria provided the team on the way to the game. There's only so much pizza you could eat, unless of course you are nineteen.

The bus with the Colonials logo emblazoned on either side glided into the lonely parking lot. It was precisely 11:05 p.m.

"Ten minutes," Coach Pete Thomas shouted to nobody in particular as he made his way off the bus to get to the bathroom before anyone else.

While all thirteen of the women's basketball players made their way to the McDonald's line to get their various snacks, Jay opted for the "healthy" choice and the shorter line at the gas station side of the rest stop. A Diet Coke, some Captain's Wafers, and some salted peanuts to drop into his bottle of soda were on the menu tonight.

James, the bus driver, was behind him with an oversized Snickers bar and the largest fountain cup available containing sixty-four ounces of Mountain Dew. James was talking about something that happened on one of the "wrasslin'" programs the night before. He always talked about "wrasslin'," but Jay wasn't in the mood for humoring him tonight to find out more that was happening in the World Wrestling Federation. Getting blown out by your arch-rival put him in a sour mood, even though he had nothing to do with the outcome. He kept the scorebook and called the scores in to the local media after the game and gave instructions to his graduate assistant about how to post the information on their brand-new athletics web site.

"This internet stuff is really taking off," Jay thought to himself on many occasions.

Jay accepted his change from the cashier, stuffed the bills back into his wallet, and dropped the nickel and four pennies into his front pocket, rubbing the one penny with the rough spot on the face of it between his thumb and index finger as he kept his hand in his pocket.

Outside, Coach Pete stood by a trash can, hastily licking a soft serve vanilla ice cream cone with sprinkles. His tie was loosened all the way down to the second button of his sweat stained yellow dress shirt, and the top button was long since undone. Roger, the radio guy, stood beside him saying nothing. He wore a grim look on his face as he looked down through his thick glasses. Roger and Pete were about the same age, in their late forties. The coach played with his mustache in between licks. He twisted some of the hairs while clinging sprinkles he didn't know were there fell to the pavement.

Outside the back of the bus Casey sat on the bumper, smoking a cigarette, and hoping nobody could see her. Everyone could. She didn't have a good night. None of them did.

Coach Pete looked back over at Jay.

"Remind me to make her run extra tomorrow for smoking," he said as he pulled a pack of Marlboro's out of his brown sport coat. "I'm too tired to fuss at her tonight."

After a pause, he continued.

"Damn bitches," he said, looking at nobody in particular.

"Penny game?" Jay asked, trying to lighten the mood.

Coach Pete gobbled the rest of his ice cream and stuck a cigarette in his mouth, almost all in one motion.

His left eye squinted as the cigarette illuminated. Nobody said a word, but Jay, Coach Pete, and Roger each fished through their pockets searching for coins.

"1995," Coach Pete said, reading the date on his penny. "Hasn't been a good year so far. "I hope I don't find this one again."

When each was satisfied with what they had found, the three faced each other, about two feet apart. Coach Pete chuckled as he tossed the first penny straight into the air.

"Can't move or you're out," Coach Pete said with another chuckle.

Reflexively the three men pulled their shoulders in as if wincing at an expected large weight to fall upon them. A moment later the clinking sound of the penny was heard five feet away from their circle.

"Nice toss Alice, can your husband play?" Jay quipped.

"Your turn," he added, looking at Roger.

Again, the three men winced as the penny came down and didn't hit any of them, but actually landed in the center between them.

"Ohhhh!" the trio laughed in unison.

Tamarra and Andrea, the two post players on the team, shuffled past as they exited the store in the matching white and gold warm-ups.

"Coach, why you guys always play that stupid game?" Tamarra asked.

"Do y'all even have any rules?" Andrea asked, but not really stopping for an answer.

Jay's turn.

He felt the rough surface of the penny as he pulled it out of his pocket. "1943 D," he said to himself, reading the front of the coin and feeling the imperfection once again on Lincoln's nose.

High in the air it went. The shoulders all pulled in, and the penny glanced off the side of Coach Pete's head on the way down.

They all howled. Coach Pete cackled as if it was the funniest thing that had ever happened. Losing three straight games, he needed to feel good.

"Does that mean I win or lose?" he chuckled.

"Tonight, it means you win," Roger exclaimed.

"Ah, man, if it wasn't against NCAA rules, them bitches would be doing wind sprints in the parking lot tonight," Coach Pete said, exhaling a big cloud of smoke from his now very ashy cigarette.

"How many turnovers did Casey have?" he asked himself, fumbling for the crumpled box score in his pocket.

"Seven," Jay said without looking as he picked up two of the pennies off the pavement from their recent game.

Jay fished another penny from his pocket. He gave one to Roger and one to Coach Pete. He kept the one with the chip on Lincoln's nose for himself.

"One more game before they all get back on the bus," Jay said.

Standing five feet from the curb, Jay explained the rules for this one.

"Closest to the curb without hitting it has the biggest dick."

"What have I got to lose?" said Roger. "I'm Irish."

The trio was always making up penny games on road trips. There were very few rules. Sometimes there weren't any.

Roger's throw was poor and hit off the curb. Coach Pete's landed about six inches shy of the curb.

Jay rubbed Lincoln's rough nose one more time and underhand tossed it to the curb. It bounced and rolled on its edge toward the curb. Jay cheered it on as it passed Coach Pete's penny, but then lost momentum, banked to the right, and rolled back about eight inches from the curb.

"Ho-ho, maybe we should have played this before the game and things would have been different tonight," Coach Pete said, taking satisfaction in his victory.

"Damn bitches," he muttered again as he picked up his prizes.

Walking toward the bus, Coach Pete fished a loose dollar bill and all the change in his pocket. He saw the homeless man with the trash bag full of aluminum cans, fishing empties out of the garbage can next to the bus.

"Here, my man," Coach Pete said as he handed him the cash.

The homeless man with his nappy beard, torn Dickies and gray eyes nodded, but didn't smile as he accepted the cash, quickly stuffing it in his pocket, then pulling it back out to see how much it was.

Walking toward the glow of the lights of the restaurant, the rough surface of one of the pennies felt good in his dirty and sticky hands. Hootie and The Blowfish sang "Hold My Hand" as he swung the door open.

"This is my lucky night," he said as he eyed the menu to see what he could afford with his new income.

OMAHA, NEBRASKA

Greg Springs was enjoying the moment in the on-deck circle. He almost didn't want it to end. It was the first game of the College World Series, and he and his Cinderella team had reached hallowed ground for the first time in school history.

They weren't supposed to be here. There were many times when he thought he wasn't meant to be here. Heck, he was told as much, too.

As he bent down to rub some of the sacred dirt from Rosenblatt Stadium on his hands, he went back in time, four years earlier when his college baseball career almost didn't happen.

"Let's go!" Assistant Coach Tony Pittacco yelled as the dozen walk-on candidates ran poles, a sprint from the right field line to the left field line and back again. Greg was working hard but was still towards the back of the pack in the sprint. He had been one of the best players on his small high school team, but he didn't get any large college scholarship offers. He could have played at a junior college in his hometown, but he always wanted to go to State.

He knew that every college baseball team had a number of walk-ons due to scholarship limits, but most of them were preferred walk-ons, which he was not. Still, Head Coach Tommy Dawson always liked to find one diamond in the rough each year to try and develop and also give kids hope.

Coach Pittacco didn't see the need for someone who likely wouldn't help the team much, if at all, so he was the "bad cop" at the tryouts.

Greg lamented his thick thighs as he tried to keep up. He was diabetic and always seemed to sweat ten-times more than the next guy.

"Let's go, Springs, pick it up!" Pittacco yelled again.

Back in Omaha, Greg took a deep breath as his teammate, Ronnie Miller, strode into the batter's box to start the game. The opposing pitcher had a full beard and looked like a grown man. Greg had seen some tape of him pitching before. The six-foot three, muscular right hander had a big fastball and a mean slider. The first pitch hummed in at 97 miles per hour for a strike and Greg whistled without realizing it.

At his walk-on tryout, Greg was getting a sip of water after his batting practice session. Dawson and Pittacco were discussing the possible newcomers and didn't pay attention to him.

"The guy doesn't belong here," Pittacco pleaded. "He's chubby and slow, and we don't need another outfielder. He can't hit for power either. Let's at least keep a pitcher in case we need someone to chew up an inning somewhere."

Greg knew he was talking about him. He wondered if he belonged and carefully stepped away.

"This kid wants it," Dawson said with a smile. "He's got a decent arm, and his swing is natural. Plus, he's a lefty."

"Start us off, Ronnie!" Greg yelled from the on-deck circle as the big right hander prepared to deliver again.

"Strike two!" The umpire bellowed as another fastball buzzed the outside corner.

Greg stood in the locker room, gazing into the mirror as he put on his State hat and his official team practice shirt. Despite Coach Pittacco's objections, he had made it. The others had been cut, and he was in his second week of officially being part of the team. Every day of getting dressed was like a dream.

He ran out onto the field, and he and his teammates started their lap around the field to warm up. Coach Dawson always joined them on the run. Some of Greg's teammates were starting to warm up to the new guy, but it was Dawson who always looked out for him.

"How's it going, Greggy?" Dawson said as he jogged alongside him.

"I'm good, Coach. Just trying to get better."

Greg watched Ronnie take a high fastball for a ball. "That was a tough one to lay off," he thought. He looked back into the dugout and Coach Pittacco was spitting seeds as he shouted encouragement to Ronnie. He had grown to love "Coach P," even if he didn't originally want him on the team.

"One more lap," Coach Dawson shouted.

Greg pushed ahead toward the front of the pack. He was actually moving up to the front, then he noticed some of the guys were slowing down or had just stopped all together. He turned back to see what he had missed.

Coach Dawson was laying on the outfield grass in a heap. Some of the other players were already running toward him. Greg sprinted faster than he ever had before.

They rolled him over on his back. His eyes were open, but he wasn't there. Greg immediately yelled, "Call 911! Get the trainer!"

Whipping off his State baseball cap, he listened for a heartbeat. Hearing none, he began CPR. It seemed like hours, but it was probably only a couple of minutes before the athletic trainer had arrived and took over. Ambulance sirens could be heard in the distance.

Greg stared down at his coach who seemed to be staring back at him, but he wasn't really. Coach Dawson was already gone.

Greg didn't see ball two miss low on Ronnie to even the count. When Ronnie fouled off the next pitch, he instinctively collected himself as cheers came from the dugout.

"Hey, that-away kid!"

"You're on it, Ronnie!"

Greg was in the waiting room at the hospital with his teammates when, Coach Dawson's wife, Hillary, came in. Tears streamed down her face and her eyes were bright red. "He's gone," she said in disbelief.

Dawson was only forty-five and didn't have any previous issues. At least nothing documented, but his heart basically ruptured. At least that's what they were told.

The small town around the university was devastated. Everyone knew Coach Dawson. He was one of the good guys. There was a process of mourning, and Coach Pittacco was named interim head coach that year. They had a good team, and they all played with a heavy heart and his number 43 was stitched onto their jerseys that year. Coach Pittacco even changed his number to 34, the reverse of 43 as a sign of respect and that Dawson would want them to move forward.

The team did well that year - finished second in the conference and just missed the NCAA Tournament. Greg ended up being a regular pinch-hitter and even started a few games in right field toward the end of the year.

Ronnie fouled off another fastball, and the big right-hander on the mound looked annoyed that he hadn't retired him yet. The next pitch came high and tight as Ronnie's eyes got as big as saucers.

"That was a purpose pitch," Greg thought.

Ronnie stepped out of the box, took a deep breath, and stepped back in the box. The next pitch was another fastball, right down the middle, and Ronnie couldn't come close as he swung and missed for strike three.

"That's alright, Ronnie," Greg said as they bumped forearms while they passed.

"Do you think you can give me more this year?" Coach Pittacco asked Greg before his sophomore year. "We've got a big hole to fill in right. You've got the arm, but I need you to produce more with the bat."

"I won't let him … you down," Greg said.

He didn't. Greg quickly became a big contributor hitting in the bottom half of the lineup his sophomore year. He hit over .300 and was fourth on the team in RBIs. Like his freshman year, he didn't hit a home run and had only a couple of doubles, but he sprayed the field with line drive singles.

"Smile," Greg's mom said as she snapped a photo of him and Coach P after he had earned the Most Improved Player award at the team banquet. Even better, Coach P had given him a half scholarship.

Greg heard his name called over the loudspeaker at Rosenblatt and strode into the left-handed hitter's box. Left foot. Right foot. Look at the pitcher.

The big sasquatch spun the ball in his right hand as he looked in for the sign.

"You almost had it. Heck, you almost had them both," said Scott, the speedy centerfielder.

It was the last game of his junior year. Greg was about to become the first player in program history to hit .400 in a season. Coach P had offered to pinch hit for him in his final at bat because his average was right at .400. The team had suffered a ton of injuries and would not be making the postseason this year.

Greg wanted to hit anyway. He didn't want a record by sitting out and not helping his team. Coach Dawson wouldn't have gone for that either. Plus, the team was down a run in the ninth. He got a hold of one pretty good. It was headed towards the gap in right center. This had a chance to not only be a game-winner, but also his first career home run. The perfect end to a tough season.

The right fielder sprinted to the warning track, put his hand on the wall, leapt up and pulled the ball back over the fence to end the game.

Greg had just rounded first, and his shoulders slumped. No win. No home run. No batting average record as he now dipped just below .400.

Greg laughed as the big righthander stared him down. He was laughing about that game from a year ago, but the big guy on the bump didn't understand. The first fastball buzzed inside, but Greg didn't flinch.

Ball one.

Greg was leading the team around the field on the first day of fall practice. Although it was a struggle, he was determined to have a good pace. Now his senior year, he thought about how quickly the years had passed. A pre-season All-American, he was now the leader on the team.

He thought about the walk-on tryouts. Every year, when a walk-on made the team, he made it a point to help him out. He thought about how Coach Dawson never got to see him develop into the player he had become. He and Coach Pittacco had a good relationship, but Greg was always dismayed that he wasn't able to show Dawson that his confidence in him was justified. That pushed him harder, and he picked up the pace as the others followed.

Greg settled back into the batter's box and stared into the

eyes of the behemoth on the mound. The two squinted at each other. Neither wanted to blink.

Greg was guessing fastball. He guessed right. Locked in, he started his swing. It felt good.

But he didn't hit it. Swing and miss. Strike one. Greg stepped out with one foot and saw the pitch had registered at 97 miles per hour.

"Nice," Greg thought, and he took a deep breath.

He wasn't accustomed to having so many microphones in his face. The local newspapers and a couple of area TV stations occasionally asked for an interview after games, and he was accustomed to speaking with the team's radio play-by-play guy, Scott.

This was different. Two days before the opening of the World Series, and there had to be more than a dozen reporters all wanting to talk to him. There were lots of different questions. Some about baseball. Some about his hobbies. Then the inevitable question came.

"So, Greg, you've had a storybook career, going from walk-on to All-American and one of the best hitters in the game," the reporter opened. "Now you're in the College World Series. With all that you've accomplished, Major League scouts don't have you high on their list because of your lack of power, do you feel like you have something to prove because you can't hit the long ball?"

Greg smiled gracefully at the question. He was well aware that he had never hit a home run. He looked at the reporter and smiled again. "Maybe I'll hit one out here for him."

Some of the reporters didn't know who "him" was. Some did. Some thought he said "them," as in, "for the scouts."

After the press conference, Greg went back to his hotel room for a nap. Stopping by the Coke machine, he fiddled with some change. A penny lay face up on the floor. A smile came to his face as he read the 1943 D date stamp.

"Huh," he marveled satisfactorily at the irony. Then he chuckled as he remembered the first part of the childhood rhyme. "Find a penny, pick it up...."

Greg watched a slider miss outside and then another electric fastball missed low. It was now three balls and one strike. Greg smiled because he knew he had the big guy where he wanted him. He didn't like to walk anyone, and with nobody on base, Greg was sure the guy wasn't worried about giving up a single.

The bearded one on the mound wasn't scared of Greg Springs. The catcher didn't even need to flash a sign.

"Time," screamed the home plate umpire as a beach ball made its way into the outfield.

The left fielder playfully picked it up and threw it back over the wall as the grateful fans cheered blissfully.

Greg locked in again and had his usual smile as the big ugly stared in, stone-faced.

The noise of 20,000 fans disappeared and the game slowed down for a moment.

The reddish/brown solid was on its way and Greg had already made up his mind to swing.

The ball exploded off his bat on a line heading towards right field. Greg immediately took off. He didn't need to pick up his first base coach to know that this would easily be a double. He hit the bag at first and made the perfect turn to second base. Out of the corner of his eye, he had seen the right fielder hustle over to the warning track to pick up the ball that had caromed off the wall.

Feeling like he could fly, he forgot to pick up his third base coach and prepared to slide into second base. He went feet-first into the bag and made it safe without a tag as a cloud of dirt rose above him.

He looked up at the base umpire, who had a grin on his face and was twirling his right hand in the air. "Keep going, son."

Confused, Greg looked up to the right fielder picking up the ball which had caromed not off the wall, but off the glove of a fan in the first row and back on to the field. He tossed the home run souvenir to the gleeful spectators.

Still in disbelief, Greg looked at the big, bearded pitcher, whose hands were on his hips, now staring disgustedly at him.

Then the noise of the crowd hit him, and he looked at his dugout where all his teammates were in a frenzy hanging over the rail, pointing and screaming at him.

Greg stood up without dusting himself off and rounded the final two bases at a good pace. He hadn't done this before, so he didn't really know what to do.

A tear came to his eye as he made sure to step on home plate, gave a forearm bump to Max, who was up next, and was swallowed by his teammates in the dugout.

He wasn't supposed to be here, but now he finally knew he belonged.

NEW YORK CITY

"Are you OK, Sir?" the attractive blond hostess asked as Joe stood frozen outside of the restaurant's bathroom he had just exited.

Joe Tenet barely heard her. He was calculating, as he liked to call it. He wasn't doing any math in his head, but it may as well have been advanced calculus for the number of thoughts and solutions that passed through his mind in a matter of seconds. No details ever escaped him.

"I'm fine," Joe said, managing half a smile but not looking at the hostess as she moved on. Reflexively, one portion of Joe's brain noted her dark grey pants suit with black pin stripes and the scent of her perfume. He always took more mental notes in case he needed it later. That's how he made it this far.

Joe Tenet didn't get flustered. He was always quick on his feet. At only sixty years old and living comfortably in semi-retirement, Joe didn't get where he was by cracking under pressure. He thought that this day would come at some point; the day where his past would catch up with him, but he never knew quite how it would happen or how he would have to own up to it.

Stepping behind a pillar to his left he was glad his favorite restaurant in Manhattan had low lighting and it was dark outside. It would be easy to just walk out the front door and be done with it. Issue over.

Unfortunately, the woman seated in the far-right corner of the room was more than just a date. This was the "one." Already divorced twice, Carolyn was almost twenty years his junior, but more than his equal between the ears, not to mention a stunning, fit beauty who really knew how to take care of him. She knew everything about him, except the one secret he never got around to telling. The ring in his left pocket was burning a hole through his perfectly pressed pants. Tonight was supposed to be the big night.

"Oh, this could be big," Joe thought as he slowly brushed his hand across his face as if to wipe away any bad ideas.

No, he had to go back. She wasn't the problem. Marty Steinbaum was the problem. Marty was a good guy. They were the same age. Both native New Yorkers who were born about a mile apart in the town of Little Neck, Long Island, but Marty's family moved to the Midwest when he was a kid, so they never crossed paths until the early 1970s through business.

Joe shook his head as he watched Marty and his overly made-up wife Ruthie, a fellow Long Islander of the Jewish faith enjoy their drinks. Marty was a character. He was loud and inappropriate, but somehow always got away with saying the wrong thing at the wrong time because of his infectious comedic personality. Marty could wear you out because he was always "on," but you had to love him. In his early sixties as well, Marty still thought he was twenty-two years old. His hair was still slicked down on his head with a definable part as always, pasting his hair from right to left across the top of his head. He still wore the same ankle high black dress boots he had worn since the 1960s. The heavy wool sport coat was just as old, but still in good shape.

Marty was loud and couldn't sit still. There were lots of big hand gestures and eyes practically spinning out of his head even as he described the simplest story from his daily routine.

Marty was a good guy alright, and Joe appreciated a good business relationship with him for more than two decades. But tonight, Marty was a problem. Marty was a problem because he lived in Detroit, not New York. What's worse, Joe Tenet was not Joe Tenet to Marty Steinbaum. Marty knew him as Dean Bennett. He's only known him as Dean Bennett. And this was a problem because Dean Bennett had been dead for more than six months.

Joe started his business in the early 1960s. It was pretty much a "me, myself and I" business. Other than a secretary and occasional part-time help, Joe's sales reach quickly stretched from the burrows of New York to New Jersey and Connecticut and within a few years was heavy in the Midwest. In order to secure these contracts early on, he had to make his company seem bigger than it was. Dean Bennett came along in a moment of pure genius. His first contact over the phone with Marty in Detroit went well from the get-go as the discovery they had both grown up in Long Island led to Joe's cold-call becoming an opportunity for a meeting. But Joe couldn't exactly have the CEO and president, himself, acting as the average sales representative by catching red-eye flights. While chatting up Marty, which really wasn't difficult because there were no short conversations with Marty, Joe eyeballed his record collection which sat beneath an antique Victrola in his office. Albums by Dean Martin and Tony Bennett jumped at him simultaneously, and Dean Bennett was born.

"I'll tell you what, Marty," Joe said over the phone. "I'll send my best guy, Dean Bennett out on Thursday to meet in your office if you can give him an hour, and we'll get this deal done."

Marty agreed, and the rest was history. Soon, Dean Bennett was making deals all across the country. Nobody outside of the tri-state area ever met President and CEO Joe Tenet, but they did meet with Dean Bennett.

Dean Bennett literally had a life of his own. He was confident and had a thorough knowledge of the company, which impressed the clients. He also did well with the ladies when the business was done. He stuck to his favorite restaurants in every town, and even though he only visited every four months or so, they knew Dean Bennett in all of them.

While Joe would never claim that taking the next step would start an out-of-control spiral, it made life complicated, if not amusing. Thanks to some knowledge and contacts made from his days in the Air Force in the 1950s, Dean Bennett soon had a social security number, driver's license, bank account, and even a library card.

Joe and Dean managed this schizophrenic lifestyle for more than two decades, and no one was the wiser.

With the advent of the internet, technology, and Joe's desire to just slow down, he needed a clean way out to tie up all the loose ends. The best way to do it was to kill Dean Bennett. It was actually Dean's relationship with a hospital administrator in Vermont several years back that gave him what he needed to get a seemingly legitimate death certificate. He even bought a tombstone and cemetery plot with a private burial. A week afterwards, he sadly sent a letter to all of Dean's clients that he was gone. Six months later he announced he was selling off his assets once all current contracts expired, and all of the loopholes were seemingly sealed.

That is, of course, before Marty decided to come to Manhattan. Sure, Marty would come to Long Island from time to time to see family, but he never would spend the money on himself for a night on the town in Manhattan with his wife. Until tonight.

For a moment, Joe tried to figure out why he was here, but that thought was quickly erased by the thought of how he was going to walk through the restaurant back to his table to retrieve Carolyn, or even eat dinner, without Marty spotting him. There was enough camouflage with some booth partitions, plants and low lighting that gave him some cover between the two tables but staying there was too risky.

They were still looking at menus, which told him they obviously were seated while Joe was in the restroom.

Carolyn didn't carry a cell phone. Joe didn't know if Marty had one, and if he did, he didn't have his number any way. So, he went old school. Joe retreated to the bathroom and called the restaurant. When the hostess answered he asked to speak with Marty Steinbaum and described exactly what he was wearing. The challenge here would be to not only hope Marty would not be facing the bathroom when he took the phone call, but how he would rush Carolyn out of the restaurant without a good explanation. He couldn't walk out on his tab and couldn't walk out the front door where Marty was taking the phone call.

As the hostess found Marty to invite him up front to take the phone call, instinct and adrenaline kicked in for Joe. He snapped his fingers as his waitress happened to make eye contact with him while she collected someone else's drinks from the bar. He made a gesture with his hands that he wanted their check by pretending to write something in the air, while silently mouthing "make the cheesecake to go." He left the call open on his cell phone but pressed the mute button.

The waitress acknowledged with a slight nod and then tended to her drink order. Joe quickly ducked out the front door without even looking to see if Marty had begun making his way up front. Outside, Joe looked left and then right, finding an alley to his right that would take him around to the back of the restaurant. Splashing through a puddle of dirty water, Joe found his way to the delivery entrance in the back where one of the bus boys was having a smoke break.

"Hey, my man," Joe said to the bus boy as he exhaled a long stream of smoke from his Malboro in Joe's direction. "Here's twenty bucks. Hail me a cab up front and hold it there for a minute."

The bus boy shrugged, grabbed the twenty-dollar bill without even so much as a smile, and walked slowly up the alley. Joe stepped through the delivery entrance. Seeing the kitchen in full force was an intricate ballet of servers, food preparers and the main chef, Moe, weaving in and out of each other's way while carrying plates and ingredients for the next order in outstretched arms. Joe tried not to upset the rhythm and moved as quickly as he could through the swinging doors that led to the hallway of five feet that formed an "L" into the dining area.

Joe carefully stuck his head out from the wall. Marty was just now wiping his face with his linen napkin while standing up to follow the hostess and take his phone call. Carolyn was busy searching the front of the restaurant with her beautiful brown eyes, wondering what was taking Joe so long.

"Damn," Joe thought to himself, disappointed in what was to be the big night where he asked her to marry him had descended into chaos.

Joe moved swiftly past Marty's table while fishing out three crisp one hundred-dollar bills to pay his tab. He placed the cash on the table and whispered to Carolyn. "We need to go. I'll explain in a minute, but we need to go right now."

"What about our cheesecake?" Carolyn pouted. "That's the best part about this place."

"I'm taking care of it," Joe said as he hurriedly helped Carolyn with her coat.

Joe glanced over his shoulder to see Marty holding the phone against his right ear, and his finger in the other ear to try to drown out the noise from the bar. All he needed to do was go back through the back door, and then think of some story to tell Carolyn to explain their hasty exit.

Then it happened. As he placed his money clip back in his pocket and pulled his hand back, the ring popped out of his pocket and bounced underneath a pair of tables toward the hostess station, was kicked by a waitress and came to rest a few inches from Marty's feet. It all seemed to happen in slow motion.

Joe froze. Carolyn hadn't seen what happened, but now what? Leaving the ring was not an option, but neither was blowing his cover.

"I've got a cab waiting up front," Joe told Carolyn, carefully shielding his face with her body from where Marty was standing.

Hearing nobody on the other end of the line, Marty had now put the phone down. He took one step and felt something under his foot. Picking up his low-cut black boot, he saw a ring. His sans-a-belt pants groaned as he squatted down to pick it up.

For a brief moment Joe was sure the cheap bastard would put it in his pocket and either sell it or give to his wife as a gift, pretending it was his own. Instead, Marty walked forward, finding the hostess at the front corner of the bar to see if anyone had reported losing the ring.

"OK, then let's go," Carolyn huffed, interrupting Joe's tunnel vision.

At this point Joe realized there's no way he could walk her out the back without a loud objection, and after all, this was

New York City. He couldn't just let her walk out the front by herself.

One last chance. He had to gamble. Ushering Carolyn in front of him to lead the way through the short maze of tables, Joe kept his head low, carefully peaking over her left ear to see if Marty still had his back to them while telling his tale about the ring to the hostess.

Joe was not an overly religious man, but growing up Catholic, he still went to church every Sunday as well as holy days of obligation. He started a short prayer to himself.

"God, if you get me through this, I'll tell Carolyn everything."

This was more for his own benefit than any sort of deal to come clean to God. He just didn't want to run into this situation again.

The waitress met them just as they passed the hostess stand. "Don't forget your cheesecake."

"Thanks," Joe said as he grabbed the to-go box without losing eye contact with the back of Marty's head. Then he bent his right leg up and in, briefly fumbled with his penny loafer and extracted the penny he had lodged in the front of his favorite shoe without missing a stride.

Marty appeared ready to turn right towards them as they were now just a few more steps from the front door. Joe deftly flicked the penny with his right hand at the waiter carrying two bowls of soup a few feet from Marty. Catching the server on the left eye of his glasses, he was startled and reflexively stepped backwards just enough, bumping into another patron followed by a quick spin, and loud dropping of the tray. French onion soup splatter and broken china diverted Marty's attention. Abraham Lincoln and his chipped nose lay face up in the melted cheese.

Joe quickly nudged Carolyn at the door with his right

hand, then hopped to his left awkwardly grabbing the ring from the hostesses' hand. "Oh, thank God, you found it," he said in a voice lower than his true pitch, bumping Marty into the messy floor as he darted out the door.

Marty spun to look at whomever had just caused him to soil his favorite shoes, but all he saw was the back of a camel colored overcoat exiting the restaurant.

Joe hurriedly opened the rear door of the taxicab, nearly falling on top of Carolyn as they tumbled into the back seat. "Central Park," he told the driver.

"What in the hell are you doing?" Carolyn protested as she tried to adjust her skirt and hair simultaneously after their less than gracious entrance.

Marty had run out of the bar and was a few feet from the taxi when the driver quickly pulled into traffic. He wasn't sure what he saw, but it didn't feel right. Staring at the cab as it went through the green light, he gave up. Pulling his pants up past his belly button, he turned on his heel to go sit with his wife.

The to-go box of cheesecake lay on the sidewalk.

"That's a shame," he said as he pulled the front door back open, greeted by Tony Bennett's "The Good Life."

BOONTON, NEW JERSEY

Darren was always a day late and dollar short. For a guy who was severely anal retentive, and borderline obsessive compulsive, Darren could just never keep it together. A careful planner and a thoughtful man of thirty-three, there was always a monkey wrench in the works or an unforeseen snag that made his life what it was. His obsessive behavior and attention to detail were sometimes his downfall; at least that's what his ex-wife told him. He couldn't help himself.

Divorced and the father of a five-year-old that he hungered to see every day, Darren was unemployed, and hadn't had what he considered a real job for three years. He held it together taking odd jobs when he could. He often held two or three part-time jobs so he could pay the rent for his little apartment, which was only a few miles away from his ex-wife and little Julia. They had all moved to New Jersey after the separation so Abbey could be closer to her family. Abbey had left him simply because she didn't love him. They only married because Julia came into the world after Darren became that guy who satisfied the .1 percent disclaimer on the prophylactic. He had no regrets about Julia though.

Abbey didn't push for child support, but Darren still sent what he could each month. Sometimes it was just a little bit of cash. For all his faults, he had a great knowledge of finance and accounting. He was meticulous in everything he did. His attention to detail was his strength, but he had a weakness for being overly trusting. That's what cost him his job at Ambrose Financial Services in Harrisburg, Pa. His former best friend, Terry, was running the business into the ground, and when cuts had to be made, Darren and his executive salary were among the first to fall.

"Today is going to be different," Darren said to himself every morning since. He was constantly in search of another position in finance, but he was always being tagged as "overqualified" for entry or mid-level positions, and there were few executive level openings within a three-hour drive of Boonton.

When he felt the first glow of sunlight on his face through his apartment window, he knew he was in trouble. Darren had set his alarm to wake him for when the sun should not have even been a glow on the horizon. In fact, his anal retentiveness had him set two alarms; one on a digital clock, and one on the old wind-up clock his mother had given him way back when he went to Penn State as a freshman. He had even checked twice to make sure he set the digital alarm time to a.m. He couldn't help himself.

Now, nearly an hour and fifteen minutes past his wake-up time, he stared in disbelief as the digital clock flashed 12:00 a.m. over and over after the power flicked off for just a moment during the night. His wind-up clock just happened to choose that night to stop ticking forever.

"Shit, shit, shit!" Darren screamed out loud as he flew out of bed.

He quickly did the calculations in his head. He could still make it to the train station which would take him to Penn Station in New York. Then it was on to the subway to lower Manhattan for his job interview. He couldn't be late for this one.

"Fresh enough," Darren said to himself, bypassing a shower.

Darren had showered after an early evening jog last night. He thought it would help him sleep. He was right about that in some regard. He tried to quickly shave what little stubble he had. His baby face skin allowed tiny whiskers to only grow in patches. As he dragged the razor across his chin while grabbing a clean undershirt from the drawer, he nicked himself. Then he did it again. Two red blobs grew on his chin.

His shoulders sank in a momentary feeling of defeat, but he quickly ripped small pieces of toilet paper to put on the wounds and got dressed. At least he was smart enough to have ironed his clothes the night before. He normally left nothing to chance. Peering at his watch, all seemed to be going well as he thought he was getting caught up on time. As he pulled the sock over his right foot, the big toe popped through where the golden stitch used to be.

A quick grunt was all he had time for in dealing with that. Unable to deny the urge to pee, Darren made quick work of relieving his bladder before the gurgle in his intestines told him he might need to make a longer visit to the toilet.

"No time," Darren said out loud, hoping his bowels would cooperate.

Grabbing a package from the box of cherry frosted Pop Tarts, Darren didn't have time for coffee. "Besides," he thought. "I'll probably spill it on my tie or shirt."

Darren was capable of making the right call now and again to keep Murphy's Law from being enforced on a daily basis.

Stealing a glimpse at his watch again, he thought about whether it would be easier to just drive into the city. It was less than sixty miles, but traffic was too unpredictable. Public transportation was still the safe way to go. It was a short ride to the train station. He opened the car door, threw the Pop Tart on the passenger seat, and was set to go.

"Shit, my briefcase," Darren said through clenched teeth realizing in the nick of time that he had set it down outside his front door as he picked up his morning newspaper. A creature of habit, sometimes he just couldn't help himself when it came to his routine.

Slamming the car door, he quickly stomped to retrieve his briefcase, and took a couple of jog steps back to the car. He felt the panic as he pulled on his now locked car door and seeing the keys dangling from the ignition. He felt the blood rush from his face, and he thought he might pass out.

Darren's bowels reminded him they had not been relieved as a slight gas pain worked its way down, adding to his folly.

The sound of Michael firing up his Kawasaki two doors down caused Darren to spin 180 degrees. He sprinted over to his neighbor, whom he didn't know all that well, but these were desperate times.

"Hey!" Darren screamed while flailing his arms and running toward the motorcycle. "Wait! Wait! I need your help. I need a ride to the train station. I've got a job interview in the city, and I just locked my keys in the car."

"Why'd you do that?" Michael asked in his monotone voice while putting on his black helmet.

Michael was not an overly kind person, and not exactly quick on the up take.

"Please, just give me a ride," Darren pleaded. "It's only a few blocks."

Darren pulled out a crisp twenty-dollar bill as collateral. Grabbing the bill, Michael jerked his head back toward his shoulder, indicating it was OK for him to hop on. Darren took an extra second to neatly arrange the other bills in his wallet. He was in a hurry, but sometimes he couldn't help himself.

Placing his briefcase in one of his saddle bags, Darren

hopped on and began to anchor himself by placing his arms around Michael.

"Uh, no," Michael deadpanned. "You may be riding 'bitch,' but you need to hold on in the back."

Embarrassed, Darren uncomfortably reached behind him and held on for dear life as Michael engaged the throttle and sped into traffic.

Darren's nicely combed hair quickly became a poofy pompadour. He was thankful that Michael was making good time to the train station, but at what cost? The two toilet paper splotches which were bandaging his rough shave had flown off almost instantly, and because he had tucked his head to look down during the ride, he now had two red ovals on his previously perfect white collar.

Upon arrival, Darren quickly hopped off the motorcycle.

"Thank you," Darren said, somewhat out of breath while looking at his watch.

Michael gave a salute and began to take off. It was then that Darren remembered his briefcase. It was still in the saddlebag.

Darren broke into a sprint as he chased the motorcycle which was moving relatively slowly through traffic. He was close to losing him for good when the enforcers of Murphy's Law took pity on him and allowed the traffic light to turn red.

Racing as fast as he could to make up the ground before the light changed again, Darren ran between the slowing cars. Horns honked. Curses flew. He finally caught up to Michael, and out of breath, he retrieved the briefcase.

"Oh my, gosh," Darren wheezed in another fit of panic as he again looked at his watch.

His train was leaving.

Ignoring the pain in his lungs, Darren made a beeline back to the train station. Just before the station, a taxi pulled in front of him. Channeling his inner "Dukes of Hazzard," Darren leapt sideways on the hood, hoping he could slide across the car and land on his feet without missing a beat.

Murphy was off from his coffee break now, and Darren ungracefully rolled across the hood, leaving a dent before flopping onto the pavement and slightly splitting his pants up the back side. Upon landing, he almost did more than *split* his pants.

As he reached the platform, Darren was now sweating through his suitcoat, and he needed to visit the restroom. The doors on the train were beginning to close, and Darren wedged his briefcase between the doors, which clamped down hard, leaving two dirty black rubber marks on the brown leather bag.

Darren let out a deep sigh. He was going to make it.

Now he had some time to regroup and perhaps take care of other business. Naturally, the train car he had entered did not have a restroom. As the New Jersey transit train made its way past the Towaco and Lincoln Park stops, Darren passed through five cars before he finally found one with a restroom. It wasn't vacant, and the current occupant was apparently having some intestinal distress far worse than Darren based on the noises he heard emanating from behind the folding door.

Darren opted to keep moving, and two more cars down the line, he found a vacant lavatory. It was vacant for good reason. The smell when he opened the door almost knocked him down. The pungent odor of urine was thick, as if a herd of livestock had all relieved themselves in the tiny room and didn't restrict themselves to the commode.

The gurgling and pain below his bellybutton told Darren he had to do it now or else something would happen that hadn't happened since preschool. The relief he felt made him briefly forget how disheveled he had become in addition to how hot and smelly the confines of the lavatory were. His bliss quickly evaporated as he turned to grab toilet tissue only to find there was none. He quickly looked up toward the sink. There were no disposable hand towels there either.

Always the survivor, Darren came up with options. He could use one of the several copies of his resume to do the job, but he wasn't sure how many he would actually need for the interview. Seeing no other alternative, he grabbed the hand-kerchief from his suitcoat breast pocket and finished his business.

He tried to wash his hands, but not only were there no paper towels, the water wasn't working either.

With as much dignity as he could muster, Darren straightened his tie and walked out of the lavatory and grabbed a seat. He felt dirty.

After several more stops, he finally stopped sweating by the time the train reached Penn Station. For all of his misfortune, it was a miracle he made it this far. He was still on time.

Upon arrival at Penn Station, Darren was famished and feeling dehydrated. He checked the times for the subway lines that would take him where needed to go. He could take the A, C, or E lines and get there, but a friend had told him the E-line was the best, so that's what he would do. Darren double checked to see the difference in the various express trains and the ones that made local stops.

He had a few minutes to spare, so Darren grabbed two bottles of water and a Nutri-Grain bar from the news stand. He counted his change to be sure he had received the proper amount. He counted twice. He couldn't help himself.

Darren chugged the first bottle of water as he reached the platform, spilling some on his tie, but not worrying about it.

"It'll dry," he thought.

The incoming subway train made his newly groomed hair fly all out of place once again. He didn't care. He was still on time. This was going to be the day. Holding his change in his right hand, he thought about getting some gum or some mints to freshen his breath.

A large crowd had gathered on the platform by the time his subway train slowed to a halt. In the rush of people coming and going, someone bumped him from behind causing his briefcase to escape his grasp and scattering the change by his feet. Reflexively, Darren tried to scoop the pens, pad, and other items from his briefcase back where they belonged with one hand, while trying to pick up his coins with the other. He dropped bits of change several times and continued to retrieve them. Darren dropped the last penny one more time, and he just had to reach back down and scoop up old Abraham Lincoln with his chipped nose. He couldn't help himself.

That's when the E-train began to pull away.

"No, no, no," Darren screamed as he pounded the glass doors of the train slowing pulling away. A woman with a nose ring and pink hair and a man in black suit both stared at him without emotion on the other side of the glass.

Darren was no longer on time. Frantically, he looked for other options. The next train that would get him close was only four minutes out, but it wasn't an express. He was supposed to be in the reception area on the 93rd floor at 8:45 a.m. sharp. He had wanted to be there 15 minutes early. Now he wasn't even going to be on time.

He cursed himself for picking up the change. He began having a fit, screaming and gesturing as if he was arguing with somebody else.

"This is why Abbey left you," he snarled. "You just can't fucking let things be! Why can't you just be a fucking normal person?! I'm running late because of fucking spilled change?"

Tears welled up in his eyes as he thought about hurling the change in his hand onto the tracks, but he didn't. He couldn't help himself.

Four minutes later he was on a local train which seemed to make one hundred stops, and none of them were his. He cursed out loud at every stop, causing an elderly woman to leave her seat and move further down in the car.

Still cursing himself as he finally reached lower Manhattan, Darren took two steps at a time coming up the steps from the subway and into the bustling city. It smelled like burnt pretzels. The bottom of his briefcase was now wet from Darren's carelessness in tightening the cap on the water bottle, rendering all of his resumes into a pulpy mess.

As he dodged businessmen and women on the sidewalk just two blocks leading up to the North Tower of the World Trade Center, Darren cursed one more time as his watch told him it was now 8:46 a.m., and he was late.

The sound of American Airlines Flight 11 slamming into the tower in front of him caused Darren to drop his cursed briefcase for the final time, while his clenched right hand finally relaxed, spilling dimes and pennies to the pavement.

For once, Darren left a mess behind, running without a destination. He couldn't help himself.

WASHINGTON, D.C.

Aariz's secret was burning a hole in the front pocket of his backpack. He couldn't wait to unleash the plan that had been worked out over the last few weeks. Having been in the U.S. for less than a year, the twenty-five-year-old was amazed how quickly it all escalated.

He hopped on the red line for the MetroRail in Forest Glen and found a seat next to a middle-aged man in the rear of the train. The man had no interest in sitting next to someone with olive skin and a beard, so he stood up, folded his newspaper, and walked to the next car.

Aariz wasn't surprised. He had become accustomed to this, but he didn't care. He was on a mission. For a moment he thought about whether he should have shaved. This would have been the right time to do it, and he had always done his best to fit in. Aariz's khakis were a little worn, as was his blue button-down shirt. He had made some sacrifices, but after today, it would all be worth it. He was tired after laying awake most of the night thinking about what he would be doing, but he felt ready.

Aariz patted the front of his blue backpack to make sure it was still there. He knew it was, but he became more nervous as each minute passed.

"Won't my family be proud?" he thought to himself, unable to restrain a smile.

Aariz shook himself to stop his little daydream. He needed to stay focused and pay attention to where he was. He studied the maps over and over so he wouldn't have to look at one while he made his way to the airport. There were a couple of different transfer stations where he could have gotten off to switch trains, but he opted for Gallery Place. He had practiced his route a few times, and he liked the way this timed out.

He knew he had several stops until then, and his mind wandered again. Aariz would truly be a respectable man after today. That's what his name meant, and today that meaning would be much deeper.

He watched a young couple bicker about something as they got on at Union Station. The train had become crowded after the last two stops, and he gripped his backpack tightly in front of him. Aariz felt a twinge of nerves as he searched the eyes of the people around him. Part of him wanted to jump out of his skin and tell them what he was about to do. Part of him wondered if it would all work out as planned.

He hadn't realized he was beginning to sweat from his forehead. He rubbed his eyes as the lack of sleep caught up with him for a moment.

At Gallery Place, he thought about whether this would be a better place to do it. The National Mall wasn't far from here, or he could pick any of the nearby monuments to unleash his plan.

He exited the train and made his way to wait for the yellow line rail which would take him to the airport.

He slung his backpack over his shoulder as he waited on the platform, careful not to leave it unattended. This was too important.

A small boy with light brown skin held his mother's hand a few feet away. Aariz inadvertently made eye contact with the child. The little one smiled, and reflexively, so did Aariz. The boy's mother looked over and frowned, pulling the boy further down the platform.

Aariz was getting used to the hate. It wouldn't matter after today.

"For all of the sacrifices you've made to get here, it will all be worth it," Aariz said as he looked down and whispered to himself.

His train arrived moments later. Sitting down, Aariz closed his eyes as he placed the backpack under his seat. He was a half a dozen stops away from the airport now. His nerves picked up again, so he decided to pray, and he soon found peace.

The rocking of the train caused him to doze off. His head bobbed forward causing him to jerk it back quickly as he awoke. The train was now stopped, and the doors were open with passengers getting on and off.

Aariz sprang to his feet and realized he was at his stop for the airport. He quickly moved to exit the train before the doors closed.

A woman on the train yelled after him, "Stop! You left your bag on the train!"

All heads turned and focused on Aariz, who was already ten feet from the train. A police officer, who had been standing at the doors between the platform and the entrance connected to the terminal moved swiftly in his direction.

People who were awaiting the next train cautiously backed away.

"Oh my gosh," Aariz gasped as he saw his plans nearly derailed.

The young woman didn't seem fazed by Aariz as she rushed his bag over to him.

The police officer had also arrived in his personal space.

"Sir, please open the bag," he said, staring into Aariz's eyes with one hand on the grip of his sidearm. He used the other hand to speak into his shoulder mounted walkie-talkie.

Aariz was suddenly confused, and he froze.

"It was an accident," Aariz protested. "I didn't mean to..."

"Aariz," called a woman who was coming through the sliding doors from the terminal.

"This is not how I wanted this to go down," lamented Aariz.

Janelle, his Canadian-born girlfriend whom he had known all his life growing up in Toronto after being adopted as a small child, was in the U.S. for the first time. Aariz had hoped to make a big impression, but this wasn't what he had in mind.

"What's going on?" Janelle asked as one of the two recently arriving police officers held her back.

The officers were on the scene with a bomb sniffing dog. The canine had no interest in Aariz's backpack. One of the officers asked for his identification and began to question him.

The first officer on the scene opened the bag, and after sorting through a notebook, a few CDs, and some random change including a bicentennial quarter and a dirty penny with a chip on Abraham Lincoln's face, he found the small box. Closing the bag, he handed it to Aariz, sighed, and told his partners it was OK, then stepped backwards.

Janelle had tears in her eyes in seeing Aariz's temporary detainment, but they turned to tears of joy as he pulled the small box out of the backpack and opened the top while getting down on one knee.

"I had planned to do this right when you got off the plane, but I guess you got in early," Aariz said as he felt the cool dampness of his sweaty shirt against his skin. "Will you marry me?"

FEBRUARY 2003

PADUCAH, KENTUCKY

The air was cool as Ryan stepped out of his apartment before his daily run. He rotated his arms a few times, marveling at being able to see his breath as he exhaled.

Looking at the road, he couldn't make up his mind on the route he would take today. There were two preferred routes he enjoyed that were doable but still very challenging. Each was five miles and looped him back home. The only difference was where the hills were.

To the right, the uphill portion of the run was near the beginning. To the left, the ascent was near the end. Although he ran one of them every day, they were still challenging.

Bending down, he grabbed the penny that lay on his welcome mat and allowed fate to decide.

"Heads, left. Tails, right," Ryan said softly.

Flipping the coin a few feet over his head, he caught it with his right hand and slapped it over onto his left arm.

"Left it is," Ryan said out loud, trying to be enthusiastic.

"Thank you, Mr. Lincoln," he added, while tossing the coin inside the door of his apartment before closing it.

Ryan used to make any excuse to avoid running, but his desire to save money and not have to buy a new wardrobe inspired him to get in shape. At twenty-six, Ryan wasn't obese, but having a desk job and not being as active as he used to be during his college days made it easy for the weight to pile on.

For the most part, the exercise had worked. He lost weight, and his pants fit him better. That made him happy.

What didn't make him happy was the sharp pain in his right knee. The stabbing sensation usually only lasted the first five minutes or so until he was really warmed up. Then he was able to run without a limp.

The first half mile was flat. Then there was a short incline, but it wasn't too taxing. It was on a busy road, so he had to pay attention to the oncoming traffic now that the sun was beginning to set.

Ryan ran around an icy puddle to avoid being splashed by any of the passing cars. It had happened to him before, and it made the rest of his run miserable.

Occasionally someone he knew would honk to acknowledge him, and Ryan always waved, not paying attention to who it was. By this point, he was concentrating on his breathing, making sure to breathe in through his nose and out through his mouth. There was nothing worse than having a runny nose and having to inhale cold air through your mouth. The burning sensation in the lungs made it difficult to run well when he made that mistake.

The second mile was always Ryan's favorite part of the run. It took him through a nice part of downtown and past a park. Having done this workout for a while, he looked mostly at ease, although it was taking longer for the stabbing pain in his knee to go away today.

He took his mind off it by remembering how just a few months ago, he would have to stop running and could only walk when he got this far.

"That's pathetic," Ryan thought about his former self.

Ryan attacked a short hill at the end of the park and turned right at the next cross street. The trees had long since lost their leaves and looked like black skeletons against the gray sky.

He noticed that his pace was good today, and yet he still wasn't breathing hard. This made him want to do more. Normally he would take the next right, which was the halfway point of his run, but he decided to keep straight a few more blocks and add a little more today. He knew if he went four more blocks up, then over and double back, he could add about a half mile.

"That would do it," Ryan thought.

The next mile, Ryan was in his zone and didn't even think about running or breathing. He thought about Lara at work, whom he liked. He liked her a lot and didn't have the guts to tell her. He also doubted she wanted anything to do with him outside of work. Still, he pictured himself talking to her and working up the courage to ask her to dinner. Would it be something nice like that French restaurant he had never been to? Or would it be better to do something casual? A pizza, maybe?

Ryan's thoughts betrayed him as his daydream didn't allow him to see the pothole he stepped in, causing his right ankle to bend sharply which also aggravated his already injured knee.

"Shit!" Ryan screamed loudly.

The pain was exquisite, but he didn't stop. He slowed down and was trying to run off the pain. Every step was painful, but he didn't want to quit. Regardless of the circumstances, he would be angry all night if he didn't finish his run. It had sort of become an addiction.

Ryan noticed he was breathing through his mouth now, not because he was tired, but turning his ankle had messed up his rhythm. His throat was burning with the cold air, making the run even more unpleasant.

Inhaling deeply through his nose and exhaling through his mouth, he got his breathing back where it needed to be in short order. His ankle and knee were still hurting badly, but Ryan felt like he could muscle through it.

Now into mile four, Ryan had a great sweat going. In fact, he was a bit hot in his layers with the heavy sweatshirt over his running shirt. He knew he had to dress warm to begin his run, otherwise his body would be too cold, his nose would run, and his breathing would never be right. He was warmer than he wanted to be, so he pulled the stocking cap off his head and pulled the hood from his sweatshirt back to let the heat escape from the top of his head.

Falling back into a rhythm, Ryan was uncomfortable running with the cap in his hands, so he stuck it into the pocket of his hoodie.

The pains in his knee and foot were becoming bearable as he approached the hardest part of the run: the hills. It started with a long and steady incline of nearly 100 yards. Ryan again attacked the hill, quickening his pace as the slope increased, trying not to breathe in through his mouth.

As he reached the top, he looked forward to the quick branching off to the right that led to a slight decline for about thirty yards. He slowed his pace to catch his breath as the next hill, which was shorter, approached. Reaching the top to another flat, he was excited because his mission was almost over. The bad news was the last leg was the toughest.

Ryan saw the long straightaway leading up to the quarter mile incline. Mindful of the potholes in the road, he passed the mobile home on the left where the pit bull lived. It was a big dog. Muscular, with clipped ears, mostly black fur, and a little patch of white on its chest. It was always outside, chained to a metal spike that was corkscrewed into the hard ground.

There were times that Ryan felt bad for the dog. It always seemed to be alone and outside.

Every time he ran this route, the dog took off at the first

sound of his sneakers hitting the pavement. He would hear the rattling of the chain bouncing off the ground for several seconds as the dog would sprint towards the road, then he would hear the "thung" sound of the chain fully extended and taught, snapping the dog back a few feet shy of reaching his prey.

Ryan was used to it, so he didn't bother to cross to the other side of the street, knowing the dog would never make it that far.

Right on cue, Ryan heard the familiar clangs of the chain as the dog spotted him.

"Chink, chink, chink," was heard in rapid succession in unison with the menacing bark of the big beast.

Ryan didn't even look.

"Chink, chink, chink," the chain continued to rattle as Ryan started on the incline.

"Wait for it. Wait for it," Ryan thought to himself as this was about the time he would hear the "thung" that pulled the dog back.

But there was no "thung" this time. Instead, it was still "chink, chink, chink."

Ryan looked over his shoulder to see that the dog was still running. The chain was still attached to his collar, but the corkscrewed end was now trailing as well as the big animal had finally yanked it from the ground.

"Shit, shit, shit!" Ryan said out loud, moving into a sprint.

Ryan looked straight ahead, and the top of the hill seemed to be getting further away, like a scene from a horror movie. He looked back and the dog was gaining, but it now had to scramble through a few yards of brush and trees.

Ryan's heartrate had accelerated greatly. Not a single car was driving down the road to help him.

"Shit."

Ryan was more than halfway up the hill. Just past that, he would be able to get into the parking lot of his apartment complex. He was already thinking how glad he was that he just left his apartment open when he went on his runs because he didn't like to run with keys.

Now he had to get there.

"Chink, chink, chink!" The chain was now louder than before as the dog had cleared the brush and was on the black top, racing up the hill.

His lungs burning from the cold air, Ryan was well aware of the sound of his own breathing, and the increased volume of the dog's bark as it drew closer. Somehow, he could even hear the click clack of the dog's paws on the road, even with the loud rattling of the chain.

"I need to get pepper spray. Maybe a gun?" Ryan thought for a moment.

Ryan could see the entrance to his apartment complex.

Almost there. Still, Ryan wasn't sure if he'd make it. This wasn't the movies or a Friday night cop show where those being chased could maintain top speed for ten minutes. His pace was slower than he wanted it to be. He couldn't breathe and thought he might throw up.

The dog was losing a little steam, too, but it wasn't falling behind.

Ryan reached the peak, darted to his left, cutting through the green space of his apartment complex.

The dog had found its second wind and was gaining. In fact, it was now less than twenty feet away and closing.

Ryan could see the four-feet high black metal fence in front of his building.

Racing through the gate, Ryan could feel the dog at his heels and was waiting for the bite that had to be coming on his leg or his rear end. As he pumped his arms, his cap fell out of his pocket and distracted the dog, for a much-needed half second.

Scampering up the sidewalk to his door, he turned the handle.

The dog skidded as it turned through the gate.

"Locked?!!! What the f-?!!!" Ryan screamed as he pounded on the door, assuming his roommate was now home and had locked the door behind him.

Ryan looked to his right and the dog was a few feet away, ready to strike at full speed.

"Thung!"

The dog was yanked back as the corkscrew had lodged itself around part of the metal fence and stopped him in mid-sprint.

Ryan's door opened, he pushed his roommate aside, slamming the door quickly behind him. The dog's chain released itself after the tension had pulled it taught, and he was now scratching at the door.

Ryan collapsed on floor and felt like throwing up.

"You should get a treadmill," his roommate deadpanned as he went back to eating cereal on the couch.

Ryan rolled over and addressed the scratched penny that was still laying on the floor.

"Next time, I'll pick the route myself."

CULVER CITY, CALIFORNIA

Andy liked the way his new UCLA t-shirt looked on him. He was pretty proud of himself. He was ready to start his freshman year, and he convinced his hovering parents to let him drive up from Newport Beach by himself and spend a few days on his own before the dorms opened so he could find his way.

Andy never had to struggle in all of his eighteen years. Living a pampered life thanks to his well-to-do parents, he was never really exposed to the real world. Hardship for Andy was not having gas in the new Ford Mustang he was given on his sixteenth birthday.

Still, he thought he was ready for anything the world would throw at him.

He closed the door to his room at the Circle K motel where he was staying until school started and then slung his laundry bag over his shoulder. The guy at the desk told him there was a laundromat just up the road. As he walked down Sepulveda Avenue, Andy already felt a sense of independence, even though the credit cards in his wallet were gifts from his parents.

As he walked into the laundromat, Andy forgot why he was there for just a moment.

An old Asian woman with gray hair and dressed in dingy white clothes was reading a book in one of the plastic chairs by the front window. In the middle was a serious looking black woman, teaching her twelve-year-old daughter how to fold sheets. Across from them, a middle-aged Hispanic man placed a load of dirty clothes into a large washer. His twenty-month-old helper picked up a stray sock from the floor and held it up for his father, who smiled and dropped it in the washing machine.

Near the back wall, a tired looking white woman watched the dryer, while her three daughters sat quietly. Two were reading books they had brought for their weekly visit. The youngest looked to be about four, and she was engrossed in a conversation with her stuffed dog.

The people in there all seemed a little bit dirty to him at first. All their clothes were old. While this was a normal Saturday for all of them, this was actually a thrilling experience for Andy, who had just realized he had probably been standing there in the entrance too long. Still, he tried to play it cool, as if he were a regular. As if this were no big deal.

Andy had never actually washed his own clothes before.

"How hard could it be?" Andy said to himself. "I got into freakin' UCLA. I can wash clothes."

As he walked down the first row of washing machines, an angry looking young black man cut his eyes toward Andy. He tried his best not to make eye contact and continued down to the end of the row where a washing machine had its lid up, indicating it was available.

Stumped momentarily about what to do next, he tried to remember if he had ever watched his housekeeper, Margarete, wash clothes, but nothing came to mind.

Not knowing any better, Andy dumped all of his clothes into the one washer. Reds, whites, blues, greens, browns, and blacks. He figured out how to slide the quarters into the slot, poured twice as much detergent than he needed over the top of the clothes, and just for good measure, he dumped the fabric softener on top of that.

Looking around for approval, Andy selected "Hot" for the water temperature, pursed his lips, and resumed his air of worldly experience.

Turning his back to his machine, he saw the other patrons either continuing their busy tasks or passing the time by reading, balancing their check book, and other duties that can take the time of a wash or drying cycle. Andy was unprepared for his wait time. No books. Nothing to occupy his time.

"Do I just go out and walk?" Andy thought to himself. "Wait, how long will it take before the wash is done?"

"Do not leave clothes unattended," read several signs taped on the walls.

He thought about asking someone if they would "watch" his machine while he went across the street to get something to eat, but suddenly, he didn't have the nerve.

Andy studied the other patrons and how they folded their clothes. He watched the little Hispanic child helping his father push the wheeled metal basket over to the dryers. The three little girls were helping their mother fold their clothes. They all knew what they were doing.

He turned the other way, and the angry young black man was looking at him. His eyes were halfway closed in a squint, so it was more like he was looking through him, lost in thoughts of his own. This made Andy uncomfortable. He wanted to be on his own, and show he was grown up and ready to be independent. Now he felt himself a little bit afraid for the first time, inside a laundromat.

Out of boredom, Andy walked over to the Coke machine in the corner, bought a Sprite, and drank it while leaning against his washing machine. He thought about how cool it was going to be to live on campus, meet pretty girls, and rush a fraternity. It wasn't long before the vibrations on the machine stopped. Andy hesitated in opening the lid as he wasn't quite sure if it was done.

Pulling a wheeled basket over, Andy plucked his wet clothes out of the machine while looking around at the other laundromat veterans. He did it. He washed his clothes. These people were no better than he was. He didn't notice that some of his whites now had a pinkish hue.

As he rolled his clothes to the dryer, Andy realized he spent his last three quarters on the soda and now had nothing for the dryer. He dug through his pockets and did find two dimes, a nickel, and a penny with an odd chip on the sixteenth president's face. The change machine only took one-dollar bills, and Andy had nothing smaller than a twenty in his wallet.

He didn't notice that the angry looking young black man was standing next to him after having already emptied his dryer.

"I've got about twelve minutes left on this one," the man said, nodding his head at the empty dryer, indicating it was OK for Andy to use his leftover time.

Stunned, Andy nodded and smiled uncomfortably and a little embarrassed that his troubles were that obvious, "Thank you."

Staying in a hotel by himself and getting his class schedule set made him think it would all be easy. Now he felt like a lost little boy. He used the penny to purchase a stale gumball from a machine that was easily older than he was. He walked over to the old pay phone and sheepishly made a collect call.

"Hi, Mom."

CINCINNATI, OHIO

A small puff of smoke flowed out of the barrel of the revolver as Alicia stood over the body in her bedroom. Her plaid shirt was ripped and hanging off her, but she didn't move to cover herself just yet.

Her dark brown eyes stared straight down into his, but she wasn't seeing him as her body trembled. His eyes appeared to be locked in on her, but, of course, they really weren't. He was dead.

Alicia didn't hear any sound, in part because of discharging three shots in succession inside the small bedroom without ear protection. It wouldn't have mattered as her mind was replaying everything in a continuous loop as she tried to make sense of what just happened.

Just a few minutes ago, she was walking up the sidewalk towards her duplex. There were no cars driving down the dark street which allowed her to notice the stranger's footsteps coming toward her from a good distance. The man's heavy and untied work boots clomped against the dead leaves as he approached. Then he passed and walked on. Neither acknowledged the other. Alicia winced at the strong odor of cigarette smoke on him.

For a moment, the footsteps stopped. She heard the crunch and dragging sound of leaves, which indicated that the stranger had turned around and reversed his course.

It didn't matter to Alicia that her street was not well-lit. Her friend, Haley, had just left her side to go into her own apartment a couple of blocks back. She normally felt safe. She knew a few of her neighbors, and the twenty-five-year-old was confident in her ability to take care of herself, thanks in part to her daddy, Roscoe; a retired United States Marine.

The footsteps continued at an even pace behind her, and Alicia didn't need to turn around to know it was the same individual who had just passed her. The familiar clomp of work boots was a dead giveaway.

Alicia placed her keys between her fingers, at first for self-defense purposes, knowing that a good punch to the face with keys poking out from between three of her fingers could be a devastating blow. She also knew she was only a few steps away from her front door, and she wanted to be ready to unlock it and get inside.

The man's steps quickened their pace, and Alicia matched it while feeling for her front door key in the darkness. She found the keyhole after a quick fumble, turned the lock, and threw her shoulder into the door to open it. Sliding inside her dark foyer, she quickly closed the door behind her, pressing her ear to the door to listen for footsteps, but heard nothing.

Alicia began to exhale as she felt for the deadbolt higher up the door.

She didn't get the chance to lock it. Alicia was knocked backward as the man with work boots kicked open the unsecured door. She fell back into the wall as her purse fell from her grasp and crashed to the floor. Alicia rolled to her right toward the living room.

The intruder closed the door, but it wouldn't lock after his kick.

"Help me! Somebody, please help me!" Alicia screamed,

hoping her duplex neighbor was home or that someone else might be passing in the street.

The man flipped on a light switch near the front door, turning on a small lamp by the window. Not much light, but Alicia normally didn't mind, unless she had friends over.

"What do you want?" Alicia screamed as she tried to keep herself from hyperventilating. "My wallet is in my purse. Just take it and go!"

"Oh, I'll get to that. Don't you worry," the man said as he looked Alicia up and down.

Alicia knew she needed to get past the man to run up the stairs and get to her bedroom. She could hear her daddy's voice, and she told herself, "If I can get up there, I'll be OK."

Before she could make her move, the man darted toward her. Alicia was instantly mad at herself for hesitating. She flailed at the man, missing badly, as he ducked under her swing, he wrapped his arms around her waist and threw her over the back of the couch on to her back.

He was on top of her. He ripped at her pink jacket, sending buttons flying across the room as she squirmed. He was not a large man, but still heavier than her. She landed only a glancing punch across his cheek, and he used his leverage to pin one arm with his knee and grab the other with his left hand. That left another hand free as he ripped at her flannel shirt. More buttons flew. His fingers felt rough and dry as they rubbed against her smooth brown skin. Alicia could feel that the man was in an excited state as he pressed against her.

"Fight," she could hear her father say.

His breath smelled like cigarettes as he buried his face into hers.

As he began to loosen his belt, Alicia felt some of his leverage weaken. Flinging her head forward as hard as she could, Alicia's blow found purchase. Her forehead crashed into the bridge of his nose, instantly spilling a pool of blood from the man's face. Momentarily stunned, he loosened his grip, and Alicia rolled onto the floor, found her footing and headed for the stairs.

She grabbed the railing and took the steps two at a time, almost surprising herself when she reached the top. Grabbing the top of the bannister, she flung herself through the hall toward the bedroom.

"You're dead!" the man screamed as he clomped up the stairs.

Alicia fumbled through her nightstand in the darkness, looking for the gun her father gave her. She only shot it a few times on the shooting range with him, but that was some time ago. She couldn't even remember if she had left it loaded.

It was at her fingertips when the man was on her again. He grabbed her from behind, but before he could throw her on the bed, Alicia bent forward and reached between her legs, finding the hem of the man's blue jeans by his clunky boots. She pulled tight and quickly stood up straight, sending the man flailing backwards as he released his grip. Another move that she learned from her dad. The man crashed into her desk, crushing the piggy bank that she had owned since she was a child.

The man rolled on to his stomach. Blood was still pouring out of his nose from both nostrils on to the pennies, nickels, and dimes now scattered on the floor along with broken pieces of piggy bank. He grabbed a fistful of coins and was ready to hurl them at Alicia as he got to his feet.

Alicia had found her walking stick next to the bed and stuck it straight in front of her. She normally only used it at night when she needed to go to the bathroom, just so she wouldn't accidentally fall down the stairs. The other one was thicker and lay by the front door, but this would suit her for now.

"You blind bitch," the man seethed. "I'm gonna beat you with that thing after I'm done with you."

The man made the mistake of swiping at the stick to knock it out of the way, which was exactly what Alicia wanted. It told her precisely where he was. She raised the revolver straight in front of her and squeezed three shots into the man's chest and neck.

The man's body fell in a heap and flopped on his back. Only a bloody penny was stuck to the man's hand, with Lincoln's chipped face staring at the dead man.

Alicia stood over the body as the smell of gunpowder wafted into her nostrils. She was afraid to move. Her ears were ringing.

The sound of approaching police sirens broke the silence as the keenest of her remaining senses returned.

COLUMBIA, SOUTH CAROLINA

Wyatt tried to conceal a wry smile on his face as he bent down to tie his shoe. He actually didn't need to tie the worn brown leather shoe. This was just how he would start his game. He had some time to kill before his flight left Columbia's Metropolitan Airport on the way to Charlotte, and later Boston.

As a consultant for McKenzie and Company, he spent a lot of time in airports. Not liking to read, he enjoyed playing games and betting with himself or anyone with him for that matter, on how well he could read people. Down on one knee beside his table where he had paid too much for a stale bagel with cream cheese, he eyed the three gates to his left in the small single terminal. Merrell, his curly haired partner and ten years Wyatt's senior, rolled his eyes as he sat and sipped his black coffee.

Wyatt squinted as his dark eyes scanned the monitors behind the counters. Two flights were scheduled to arrive within the next ten minutes. One was coming in from Charleston, the other from Charlotte. With all the stealth and dexterity his forty-year-old hands could muster, Wyatt pulled three coins from his pocket, held his balding head still while his eyes scanned left, then right, then left again. Assured that nobody was looking at him or was even in the sightline for him to pull off his caper, he flicked the three coins with a back-handed twist of his wrist, sending them across the cool black tiled floor. The dime slid and then stopped easily only ten feet from where Wyatt had turned it loose. The shiny nickel and the dull copper penny rolled on their respective edges almost side by side. Twenty-five feet later, as the two coins approached the gray carpet near the seating area at Gate 9, the nickel began to peel to the left, while the penny peeled slightly to the right. The nickel hopped onto the gray carpet and fell in front of the nearest chair. The penny continued its right arc, as if it were caught in a whirlpool before finally wavering to stop. Abe Lincoln's chipped nose faced up about three feet from another row of chairs.

Wyatt straightened himself up with a little bit of effort. The twenty pounds of extra girth he put on over the last ten years made him look a little sloppy as his white dress shirt always seemed to come un-tucked from his khaki pants. Feeling like he had committed the perfect crime, his eyes were quickly met by the cashier behind the café counter who had sold him the bagel.

Busted.

She twisted her lips and nose to the right side of her face with a disapproving look. Wyatt managed an indifferent smile and took his seat, facing the coins.

"Now we wait," Wyatt said as he took a large bite of his bagel – a dollop of cream cheese sticking to his cheek.

"You should read more," Merrell said without looking up from his coffee.

"You love it," Wyatt snorted with a cock of his head. "The dime goes first. I'll give you the other two. The usual: winner buys our next lunch?"

"Whatever," Merrell said, again without looking.

The passengers from the Charleston flight entered the terminal. As Wyatt sat, he was fidgeting like an adolescent hiding in the bushes having just rang the doorbell after placing a bag of flaming dog poo on the neighbor's doorstep. To his chagrin, the entire group passed. All three coins were still in play.

Merrell didn't have to look. He simply raised one eyebrow and turned one side of his mouth up in a half smile at his partner.

"Here we go," Wyatt whispered. "I'll tell you who is going to pick these up. I can read people just by looking at them. That's how I got where I am today."

More departing passengers trickled in. Several nearly stepped on the dime, but still no takers.

"These folks coming off the plane look too ready to be home," Wyatt said. "I can go ahead and tell you they're not stopping. Let's see, guy in the gray suite. Nope. He doesn't need it and wouldn't be seen picking up loose change. The guy in the blue jeans, I don't think so. His eyes are up looking for the bathroom. That woman in the pink Gamecocks t-shirt, no, she's more worried about who is looking at her."

Wyatt did this for every passenger, making excuses as to why each and every passenger would not pick up the coins. Merrell didn't protest the annoying verbal onslaught anymore.

An elderly woman with large black glasses, lime green pants and a white and yellow flowered shirt, approached from the other side of the terminal. Her posture left her slightly bent over, almost purposefully pointing her sightline down to the floor.

"OK, grandma here. She's definitely picking one up," Wyatt chirped confidently.

The woman missed the dime, much to Wyatt's dismay, but she found a seat closest to where the penny was resting. Still, she had not seen it.

"Take your time, granny," Wyatt whispered, still confident.

A large group of seventh and eighth grade students made their way from the security area into the terminal. They all donned red, blue, or white polo shirts with the Hammond School crest on the front. The four adult chaperones behind them were engaged in frantic conversation, perhaps antici-pating a long trip trying to keep nineteen youths under control. The students were all conversing but very few were actually looking at each other. Several had their cell phones glued to their ears, while most of the others had their heads buried in their phones playing some sort of game, while lis-tening to music on their Ipods. Any instructions from the chaperones would have been in vain for most of them.

At about the same time, the flight arriving from Charlotte belched more than seventy passengers into the terminal, cre-ating quite a bit of foot traffic.

The loud wail of a baby crying turned Wyatt's attention away from his game. He seemed annoyed at the diversion. It was behind him at the other side of the terminal. Even Merrell looked up.

A soldier dressed in fatigues cradled a young baby, not more than a month old. Wyatt and Merrell had not noticed when they had arrived or which way they had come from. They could not see much of his face yet as his head was turned down, quietly speaking to the child. His wife, dressed in blue jeans, white tennis shoes, and a black v-neck shirt stood beside him. Tears streaming down her face, while she had her hand over her mouth. An airport attendant stood five feet away.

"OK, genius," Merrell said sarcastically. "What's his story? Did he just get back or is he just shipping out?"

Game on. Wyatt turned to study the family, making silent notes to himself.

"Alright, the guy from the airport is there obviously be-cause the solider was or is the passenger, and I know military personnel can have family come through security even if they are not flying," Wyatt thought out loud. "But are they saying goodbye or is this a reunion?"

The soldier looked up slightly, his eyes were red as if he had been crying and either stopped or simply ran out of tears. He tried to keep his lips in the shape of a smile rather than a quiver as he asked his wife for a bottle to feed the child.

"If he was arriving, she could have met him in baggage claim," Wyatt said, thinking he had solved the puzzle. Then he saw the duffle on the floor a few feet away. "I guess he could have carried that on, too."

Again, the soldier returned his gaze to his daughter, locked in on her eyes. He rocked slightly without realizing he was doing so.

Wyatt started doing math in his head, playing with his fingers.

"OK, that baby can't be more than six weeks old, if that," Wyatt again thought out loud. "Obviously he couldn't have been gone more than nine months, so if he had been deployed, he probably would have been gone about twelve months or so?"

"I really don't know," Merrell added with a straight face.

"If I'm right, then he must be leaving," Wyatt said, convinced he had solved the puzzle.

"What if he had been wounded or reassigned?" said Merrell, keeping the game open.

The wife handed her husband a bottle, and he fed his daughter.

"Was it the first time?" Wyatt thought to himself this time. "Or could it be the last time he feeds her."

The last thought sobered him for a moment as he stared intently at the soldier's face. He continued to rock his daughter, never releasing eye contact. His wife sat beside him, placing her hand and chin on his shoulder.

Wyatt thought of his daughter, Caroline. She was nine. He couldn't bear to think about not being there when she was born or having to leave her right after she was born. Reflexively he pulled his cell phone out of his pocket to call home. He turned slightly, facing the glass windows out to the tarmac. When the answering machine came on, he remembered no one would be there. His wife was at work, and Caroline would be at school.

Merrell finally broke the silence and pulled Wyatt back into the present.

"You ready to go? We're boarding now."

"Huh? Yeah."

Wyatt turned. The soldier, the wife and the baby were not there. Where did they go? Did they go down to baggage claim? Did he board one of the other flights already?

"How long had I been standing there?" Wyatt thought to himself.

He craned his neck to look down the terminal but did not see them.

As he walked toward his gate, he remembered his original game. He spun around, his eyes darting on the floor looking for the coins. He could not see any of them. The voices in his head spoke all at once. Did they get kicked around? Did one of those kids pick up the dime or the nickel?

Like the soldier with the baby, he would never know. Was the soldier on his way to happiness with his family or months on end away from his infant child and wife? Did grandma pick up that penny? Is it in someone's pocket on one of these flights heading to some other part of the country?

"Don't worry," Merrell said, sensing Wyatt's turmoil. "You can play your game next week on the way to Detroit."

NEWARK, DELAWARE

Kelli smoothed the front of her blue skirt as she looked in the mirror. She turned to the left and to the right and liked what she saw. Kelli had already changed outfits three times and the discarded clothes lay in a heap on the closet floor.

She tried to tell herself that Terrence, the guy she had been matched up with through the web site didn't seem like the kind of person who cared what she looked like, but she wanted to make a good impression anyway.

Kelli kept smoothing the front of the dress, started walking out of her bedroom, and then backed up one more time to check her look in the mirror. She played with some hair on her forehead and used her fingers to push it back, just right.

She looked at her makeup.

"Not too much. Not too little," she thought to herself.

Taking a deep breath, she stared into her own eyes.

"I can't believe I'm doing this," she said out loud, exhaling again. "C'mon girl. People do this all the time. Just because you're forty doesn't mean you can't, too. This is a good thing."

One more swipe of lipstick and she was ready.

Kelli searched for her keys in her purse, grabbed a bottle of water from the fridge and strolled out to her car.

The ringing of her cell phone caused her to frown as she didn't want to be distracted. It was Mom, again. "Ugh, not now, Mom," Kelli said without answering.

Her mom wasn't too pleased when Kelli told her what she was doing. She said it was dangerous. Mom thought everything was dangerous for her only daughter.

She poured herself into the white Honda and pulled out of her driveway. Having mapped out her route in advance, she knew it would only take twenty-five minutes to get there. Those twenty-five minutes were fraught with second thoughts.

"Was it too late to back out?" a little voice inside Kelli asked. "Maybe Mom's right. Maybe this isn't smart. She has been right about a lot of my life choices."

"No!" she said out loud, hitting the steering wheel. "You can do this. You've played it safe your whole life. It will be fine."

Kelli repeated, "It will be fine" throughout her trip, but she hadn't fully convinced herself. She tried to remember a conversation she had with Terrence after they were matched. He seemed so happy, and so full of life. He was funny. Kelli thought he looked sort of pale in the photo he sent, but there was something about his eyes that enveloped her. They were a little sad, but also hopeful.

Sitting at a stoplight, Kelli wondered if Terrence was nervous. Grabbing her cell phone, she looked up at the light to make sure it was still red. Finding Terrence's name in her contact list, she typed, "On the way. See you soon."

Satisfied that her message was appropriate, she hit "send." The horn from the car behind her let her know that the light had changed to green. Kelli made a face in the rearview mirror at the impatient traveler behind her and hit the gas.

She couldn't get over how quickly things had progressed to get to this point. "What were the odds of finding someone so close?" Kelly thought again.

"There's no turning back now," Kelli thought as she pulled into the parking lot. She didn't like the way her purse made so much noise from the loose change scattered about, so she grabbed her lipstick and dumped the contents into the center console. A lone penny missed the mark and bounced onto her lap, but she didn't notice. "OK, let's go meet Terrence."

The penny rolled onto the pavement as she exited the car, and the imperfect 1943-coin lay face up. Kelli still hadn't noticed.

"Go through the lobby to the elevators and up to room 603" were the instructions she had been given. Kelli caught herself in a mirror as she walked down the hall. Her hair was still in place, and her skirt looked good.

Finding room 603, she knocked lightly on the door.

"Come in," came a response, almost immediately but softly.

Kelli opened the door. "Terrence?"

"You must be Kelli," said the woman, who appeared to be the same age as Kelli. "I'm Megan, Terrence's wife."

The two stood still awkwardly for a moment. A tear began to slide down Megan's cheek. One, then another, and another.

Kelli could feel the tears welling up in her face as well.

Megan shuffled over to Kelli and threw her arms around her. Kelli returned the embrace as Megan continued to sob.

"Thank you," Megan said, stepping away at arm's length for a moment. Then looking over her shoulder at her sleeping husband in the hospital bed with various tubes and wires seemingly everywhere. "He just dozed off, but I know he wants to meet you."

"Don't wake him," Kelli cautioned and smiled. "It's OK."

Terrence did look pale, but his face was still kind. There were photos of the couple's two children next to the bed. A boy and a girl. One showed a livelier Terrence posing proudly with his son after a little league baseball game. His face was fuller, and his skin had a more natural tone. Kelli couldn't get over his eyes. They were radiant! The little boy had them, too.

"You are an answer to prayers," Megan said, bringing Kelli out of her stupor. "When he was put on the kidney transplant list, we didn't think we would have any matches so soon, and then to find out you had just put yourself on the list and that you were here in the same town... well."

Megan's voice trailed off as more tears came with her just shaking her head in disbelief.

Kelli smiled and cried some more. She no longer cared about her dress and her hair. She wasn't scared anymore about living with one kidney. "People do this all the time," she thought. Then she smiled, reaching for the picture of Terrence and his children. "I can't wait to tell Mom that she's wrong about this one."

CHICAGO, ILLINOIS

Adam stared down into the amber-brown liquid at the bottom of his glass as he drank his bourbon at the corner of the bar. Soft piano music tinkled in the background as it always did.

"Are you ready for another?" Billy, the career bartender, asked.

Adam raised his near empty glass to confirm he would indeed like another drink, and then brought it to his lips to make the last ounce disappear.

"I'll get it," said MacLean, the twenty-two-year-old bartender who was just coming on for his shift.

Billy obliged and went back to washing some glasses. In his late forties, he took pride in his job. He never went to college, and he enjoyed his life. He knew his regulars well. He took care of them, and they took care of him.

Adam nodded as MacLean brought him his drink but didn't say a word. He looked at his watch, then smoothed his hand over his gray hair that was combed neatly, straight back.

"What's with the tuxedo?" MacLean whispered to Billy.

"Leave it alone," Billy said without looking at him.

Smith's was a nice restaurant. It was elegant. Coat and ties were necessary for gentlemen. Adam didn't come often, but when he did, it was in black tie. Now sixty-five and recently retired, the old black tux still fit him well. The jacket was getting a little loose in the shoulders as Adam's physique had changed in the fifteen years that he owned it. Fortunately, the pants were adjustable at the waist to accommodate changes below the navel in recent years as well.

Adam sat quietly with his drink. Every couple of minutes he would look at his watch, then take a sip, place the glass on the coaster and stare straight ahead.

"Looks like the old fella might be getting stood up," Mac-Lean remarked.

"Not quite," Billy smiled. "Look, I've got to help out with that private party in the back for a bit. Just give the guy what he wants, and just let him be, OK?"

MacLean nodded, but in his mind, he knew better than Billy. The elder bartender brushed some lint off his younger co-worker's black vest and picked a string off his white sleeves as he shook his head.

"Billy's just saying that because the old guy probably has big money, and he wants the big tip," MacLean said to himself.

MacLean fashioned himself to be an all-star behind the bar, seeing himself like the guys in the movies and television with all the answers. Always knowing what to say like "Isaac" from *The Love Boat*. Whitty, like "Sam" on *Cheers*. Cool like Tom Cruise in *Cocktail*. He didn't aspire to be a bartender the rest of his life, but the money was good for now, and he told himself it was a great way to network.

MacLean attended to a few others at the bar. Most of them were just having a drink while they waited for their table. A white wine here. A gin and tonic or martini there.

Adam continued to sip his bourbon, look at his watch, and then wait.

MacLean slid over and wiped imaginary residue from the spot next to Adam with a white rag.

"She's running late, huh?" MacLean said with a wink, insinuating that Adam was waiting on his wife or maybe a mistress.

Adam didn't move but turned his eyes just for a moment at MacLean, saying nothing.

MacLean tried to play it cool. He was leaning in on his elbow, faking a sympathetic smile. With no response from Adam, he was starting to feel awkward. He was saved by a customer at the other end of the bar requesting service. MacLean patted the bar with his hand twice in a way he thought was comforting as he walked away.

Adam found it patronizing. He watched a younger woman, perhaps thirty, walk into the restaurant with her husband. She took off her coat, and Adam was drawn to the smooth, flawless skin on her toned arms, running up to her shoulders. It reminded him of how Sheila looked many years ago. He looked at his watch again.

Ten minutes passed, and MacLean was busy with other customers, but he still wanted to win over Adam. It didn't look like he was going anywhere any time soon as Adam had turned away from the bar for a few minutes, scanning the crowd, the front door, and the crowd again. He tapped his finger reflexively on the bar as he kept time with the music. Then he took his jacket off and wrapped it around the back of his chair.

MacLean moved in, knowing there was at least another drink to be delivered, meaning more time to ingratiate himself with his formal guest. This time, he tried a different approach.

"I'm MacLean, by the way," he said, extending his hand toward Adam. "My friends call me 'Mac.'"

Adam looked at his watch again. He took the last swallow of his bourbon and placed his empty glass in MacLean's extended hand. He tapped the top of the glass to indicate he was ready for another drink but said nothing.

Strike two.

MacLean was suddenly self-conscious about whether anyone had noticed the awkward exchange. He went to pour another bourbon and decided to fill the glass a little higher in another attempt to get in with his customer.

Adam accepted the drink without a word. It was painfully obvious that he wanted to be left alone, but MacLean hadn't picked up on that clue. He was still hoping to solve Adam's problem; whatever it was.

The bar began to empty as the other patrons were brought to their tables.

MacLean looked at his watch and realized it had been more than an hour since he arrived on duty, and clearly Adam's guest was not coming. The old man never once checked his cell phone for any sort of message or text. Maybe he didn't even have one. He slid over to Adam once more, resting on one elbow once again.

"If you want my two cents, maybe you should go ahead and order something to eat," MacLean said. "It's getting kind of late, and if your guest hasn't called to let you know when they might be arriving, well, I just hate to see a fine gentleman such as yourself go hungry. I can show you the specials if you'd like."

Nothing from Adam.

"If you need to make a phone call," MacLean trailed off realizing that Adam wasn't paying any attention to him.

MacLean retreated back toward the register and watched as Adam continued his routine. A sip of the drink. A scan of the front door and the dining room. A look at his watch. A finger tapping to the music.

Billy returned with a bottle of champagne and looked a little bit tired.

"Tough crowd?" MacLean asked, referring to the private party in the back.

"Nothing I can't handle," Billy smiled. "Are you staying out of your own way here?"

MacLean pulled back as if he was offended by the remark.

"Well, it's slowed down," MacLean said and then turned so Adam couldn't see his face. "Your boy at the end of the bar isn't much of a conversationalist."

"I told you," Billy said. "Just get him his drink and stay out of his way. I'll take it from here."

Billy checked his watch as the piano player started in on "As Time Goes By."

Adam turned to Billy and put up two fingers. Billy was already pouring two glasses of Champagne. He brought them over to his guest and the two nodded at each other. There was a silent understanding. Adam put his tuxedo jacket back on to drink the champagne.

Billy turned and walked over to Maclean.

"The gentleman has been coming here for as long as I can remember," Billy said. "Longer than I've been here. He and his wife used to come here once a year on their anniversary. They would each arrive separately, as if they were meeting for a blind date. Always dressed to the nines. They'd have a few drinks, then toast to their marriage with champagne. He would always request that song in advance at precisely 9:45 p.m. It was the time he asked her to marry him. They danced to the song at their wedding."

"So, what happened to…" MacLean began.

"Cancer. Eight years ago," Billy said. "He still comes back every year. Same night. Same time. Same drinks. It was her favorite place, but he won't eat here without her."

Right on cue, Adam raised his hand to signal he was ready for the check.

Billy walked over as MacLean trailed him.

Adam pulled out his wallet, placed two crisp one hundred-dollar bills on the bar and slid it to Billy, nodding to imply that no change was needed.

"Thanks, Billy," Adam said, speaking for the first time.

MacLean looked slightly annoyed that he was not being rewarded even though he had waited on him most of the night.

Adam fished a pair of pennies from his pocket and placed them on the bar; one face up, one face down. He slid them on the bar in MacLean's direction and addressed him for the first time.

"Here's my two cents," Adam said with a sparkle in his eye. "Sorry, kid, but I don't think you're very good at this line of work. You might want to try something else."

MacLean looked down in disbelief at the two coins. Abe Lincoln's chipped visage mocked him, as Adam turned to walk away.

"Darling," Adam said to himself. "We may have to find a new place next year. I think this place is starting to go downhill."

AUGUST 2013

BALTIMORE, MARYLAND

Madeline's heart was racing as she woke up gasping for air. She took a moment to catch her breath and slowly pivoted her body to place her feet on the floor as she sat up in bed. Switching on the lamp from her nightstand, she grabbed the pen and her journal to start recording some elements from her nightmare.

She had to do this before the memories of her dreams vanished or diminished, as they often did within minutes after waking. It had been several months since she started being haunted by recurring images while she slept. It was getting so bad and so frequent that Madeline finally broke down to see a psychiatrist.

Madeline thought that talking about it would make the bad dreams go away. That's what her mother had told her as a child. Mother wasn't right this time.

After opening up to a friend and later, her shrink, the nightmares continued. Dr. Lidstone had told her to start writing down any details of her dreams as soon as she was awake because the brain doesn't always keep those memories easily accessible for long periods of time.

Despite nearly thirty pages of various scribbles, drawings, and incomplete sentences about her dreams, it was all still a mystery to Madeline. Dr. Lidstone told her repeatedly that she wasn't going crazy, but Madeline wasn't so sure anymore.

"He's talking to me, but I don't hear him," Madeline spoke as she wrote the same in the journal. "I can't make out the words he is saying."

She tried drawing a picture of the blue-eyed young man in her dreams. Madeline cursed herself for not being able to accurately recreate the image in her head onto the paper. She flipped through several pages of the journal. There were many such attempts to draw, but none of them resembled the image she was seeing.

"Who are you?" Madeline thought. "What do you want?"

Madeline could feel her heart racing, and another panic attack was trying to sink in. She did her breathing exercises.

The ringing of the telephone was a welcomed distraction and helped her win this round with her mind. She didn't have to look at the clock to know it was exactly 9 a.m. Her mother, Savannah, always called at 9 a.m. every Saturday. She used to call earlier, but Madeline had to put her foot down a few years ago when her mother would call before the sun came up because she was awake and figured the rest of the world should be as well. Madeline had arbitrarily told her that it's rude to call anyone before 9 a.m. on Saturday, and Savannah took it to heart.

"Hi, Mom," Madeline said as she picked up the phone.

The conversation kept lingering feelings of anxiety at bay, which was good, but any remaining fresh details of last night's dream were also lost.

Twenty minutes later, Madeline told her mother that she loved her and hung up the phone. Madeline's home was quiet and lonely. The forty-eight-year-old was divorced. No kids. No pets. She would joke with her friends that she wished two out of three of those conditions were different, but which of the two conditions were most desired would change on a daily basis.

She brushed her brown hair until it hung neatly to her shoulders. Madeline had plain features. She was neither fat, nor thin, and there wasn't a lot of muscle definition. A regular "plain Jane" she would tell herself.

Madeline liked to treat herself by getting coffee and a pastry at the shop a few blocks from her home, and then walk to Patterson Park where she would just people-watch over breakfast. Sometimes she ran into someone she knew. Sometimes she didn't.

Although it was cloudy, Madeline could tell it was going to be a nice day. The smell of the warm muffin in her bag tempted her on her walk. She would always wait until she got to the park before taking a bite, and only allowed herself a few sips of coffee before finding a bench to sit.

She passed by the fountain and fished a penny out of her purse to make a wish. It wouldn't be the first time, and probably wouldn't be the last. She studied the dented nose on the sixteenth president's face as she raised the coin and threw it awkwardly into the fountain, wishing her dreams would stop.

She didn't have faith that her wish would come true, and the penny sank to the bottom just the same.

The park was alive this morning. An old man was walking an equally old brown dachshund. A young boy held hands with his mother while cradling a yellow ball as they walked on the grass. A group of pre-teens rode bicycles back and forth. One of the boys turned his head back to say something to the group behind him, but he seemed to be looking right at Madeline. She couldn't make out what he said but was startled back into the memory of her dream.

Madeline dropped the muffin into her lap and was able to catch it before it rolled on to the ground. She looked up, and the boys on the bicycles were now well past her, but Madeline's anxiety had caught up to her once again.

She felt dizzy and thought for sure her heart was racing. Closing her eyes, Madeline touched her neck with two fingers to check her pulse. It felt normal, but her own action was making her more anxious.

"It's all in your head," Madeline whispered to herself. "It's not real. It's not real!"

She thought about how easy it is to say, "It's not real," but for anyone suffering from a panic attack, it's very real. That was something her mother never understood.

Madeline grabbed the front of the bench with one hand to steady herself. Her shoulders began to tense up.

"Are you OK, miss?" said an unfamiliar voice.

Madeline opened her eyes. The young nun was bent over with her hands on her knees. Her cross hung down from her neck. She was in a full brown habit. Madeline was momentarily dumbstruck.

The nun sat beside Madeline, placing a hand on her shoulder.

"You were shaking," the nun said. "Do you need some help?"

Madeline suddenly felt a calming presence by the nun who was easily twenty years younger than herself.

"I thought all nuns were really old," Madeline said out loud, much to her own surprise. "Oh my gosh. I'm sorry. I don't know what happened, I was just …"

The young nun laughed hysterically as Madeline blushed with embarrassment.

"Some of us find our calling early on," the nun said. "I'm sister Anna Maria."

"Of course," Madeline said, internally this time, then a whisper. "Aren't they all named 'Anna Maria'? Oh my gosh! I don't know what's wrong with me."

Then she caught herself. "Thank you. I'm fine. I just

haven't been sleeping well. Forgive me. Where are my manners? I'm Madeline."

"Well, Madeline, I'm just visiting, and I'm here waiting for some colleagues of mine," the nun said. "I saw you shaking, and I thought I was going to have to cast out some demons."

Madeline was confused at first, but when she realized Sister Anna Maria had a grand sense of humor, she immediately relaxed, smiled, and offered her a piece of her muffin.

"I'll have to admit, I haven't been the best Christian," Madeline felt compelled to admit to her new friend. "I haven't been to church for a long time. Oh, and I'm not Catholic."

"Neither was Jesus," Sister Anna Maria quipped. "Nobody's perfect."

The two laughed like old friends, and Madeline's anxiety was long gone. Neither had anywhere to be anytime soon. Madeline sipped her coffee. Sister Anna Maria told her about her calling. It was ten minutes into their conversation that Madeline felt something profound. It was the way the young nun had explained that she had been a terrible sinner in her younger days. It was that confession that compelled Madeline to open up as well.

"To be honest, Sister, I've been having a lot of personal problems with anxiety and such. For what it's worth, sometimes I pray and that helps my panicky feelings go away. I have bad dreams. Over and over. I try to forget them, but I also try to remember them, so I can figure them out."

Madeline thought perhaps she was sharing too much. Sister Anna Maria smiled and seemed very interested, so she kept going.

"I try writing it all down and even drawing pictures of the face I keep seeing. I'm not very good at drawing though. I can't figure out who this person is, and it's driving me crazy. His eyes are so familiar, yet I don't think I've really ever seen him."

She sipped her coffee and tried to smile with a sideways glance at the nun, "Maybe I am possessed."

The young nun laughed again. "Probably not, but sometimes our sins can weigh on our conscience. That's why you have to find a way to unburden your soul."

"Can you hear my confession, even if I'm not Catholic?"

"Unfortunately, no. I'm glad to listen though, if you think it will help," the nun said as she fished out a piece of hard candy from inside her habit and held it up to Madeline.

"No, thank you," Madeline said as the nun's words about unburdening her soul repeated in her head. "Enough about me. Tell me again why you're here."

"I just came to help a friend," Sister Anna Maria said as she pulled two smooth stones from her habit.

"What else does she have under there?" Madeline thought as she laughed inside.

"This is a special place for me. Many years ago, there was a woman strolling through this park, and she came upon an old nun, Sister Magdalene Marie."

The nun paused to see Madeline's reaction to that name. Madeline's lips started to curl uncontrollably upward in a smile.

"The old nun was throwing stones into the pond. She would say a name, throw a stone, make the sign of the cross and pray a silent prayer. This could go on for a long time. Sometimes she would have a big basket of stones, and sometimes she had to get some of the other nuns to help carry them.

"On this particular day, it was cold and a little bit rainy. A young woman and her sister came upon the nuns. She saw that each stone was smooth and had something written on it with magic marker, so she asked what they were doing. Sister Magdalene Marie told the woman that in her work, she met with a lot of poor and sick individuals, and they all felt comfortable telling her things. Awful things. Sins. Things that she would encourage them to confess to a priest. Well, anyway, she told them to ask for God's forgiveness and not to burden their souls by worrying about the past if they were indeed truly sorry. She had them write their initials on the stone, and one word about their transgression that bothered them so much."

Sister Anna Maria paused to pull the small hard candy out of her mouth, studied it, and poked it back in.

"She told them that instead of casting stones of shame at themselves for what they had done, she was going to cast the stones into the water, relieving them of that burden and allowing the water to wash away whatever word that represented their sin.

"One of those two women who had stopped, burst into tears and quickly hurried away."

The nun stopped and smiled. Madeline looked confused.

"I don't understand. How does this involve you?"

"The woman who ran off crying was pregnant. She didn't have a husband, you understand? She could barely pay her rent and had just told her sister she was getting an abortion. As it turns out, she had a change of heart that day. That moment."

Sister Anna Maria paused to let it sink in.

"She was your mother!" The words escaped Madeline's mouth at the exact moment the thought entered her brain.

Sister Anna Maria smiled warmly and used her thumb and forefinger, firing an imaginary gun at Madeline. "Yep. This is where I was born, so to speak. Well, not this very park, but you see why this place is special to me. Here's the kicker, my mother's name is Petra. You know, like 'Peter,' the rock of the church?"

Madeline's mouth was agape.

"The Lord works in mysterious ways," the young nun continued with a smile. "So, I'm here to meet Sister Magdalene Marie later. She's ninety-one now, but she can still throw the stones. Can you believe that? I brought a few with me. Maybe I can change someone's life, too. Wouldn't that be something?"

Madeline was indeed touched by the story, and for a moment her mind drifted to a decision she had made many years ago that had a different outcome. She couldn't help but wonder what her life would have been like had she made the same decision as Petra. Madeline began to feel flush, as she did the math and realized her own child could have been the same age as Sister Anna Maria right now. Surely the guilt she felt must be visible, and she became very uncomfortable.

Sister Anna Maria saw her new friend was distracted, placed one hand on Madeline's, speaking softly, "I'll pray for you."

"Does she know?" Madeline thought. There was a sense of calm as well as an overwhelming sense that she needed to bare her soul. But she couldn't. Then she felt the young nun place one of her beloved hard candies in her hand.

"These are good," Sister Anna Maria assured her. "They have them at the convent, and I just can't resist."

Madeline smiled, took her last sip of coffee, and found herself standing up. "I have to go but thank you so much for stopping."

"I'll be here tomorrow as well, after the eight o'clock Mass," the nun offered.

The rest of the day was a blur for Madeline. There was something about the young nun and her story that sent her mind searching. If nothing else, it was a pleasant distraction to the usual thoughts that sent her into a panic.

She spent the day walking and thinking, often finding herself staring into space before she came back to her senses and wondered how long she had been standing in the store or on the street corner. Madeline felt exhausted and relaxed herself with a generous glass of wine and a bath after dinner.

After climbing into bed, she lay on her back struggling to find sleep. She heard the nun's voice over and over, "You have to find a way to unburden your soul."

"What does that mean?"

Several hours later, Madeline woke up from her familiar dream. The eyes of the young man were still fresh in her consciousness. They seemed more familiar to her now. She had a connection with him, but for some reason she wasn't scared of him today. Sitting up to grab her journal she closed her eyes to replay what he had mouthed to her in the dream.

"Ask and commit to him," was what she wrote in the journal as a wave of warmth spread through her chest and face. She heard his voice for the first time. A tear ran down her face as she finally recognized the young man in her dreams as the grown child she never knew. Dr. Lidstone probably wouldn't buy it and would likely want to ramp up her prescription.

She looked over at the clock. It was 8:55. Madeline dressed quickly and didn't bother with her hair. She grabbed her cell phone and for the first time in a long time, initiated a morning call to her mom as she rushed out of her home.

"Ask and commit to him."

She saw his face and heard him say it this time. What a beautiful voice.

Madeline skipped the coffee shop and went straight to the park. It was now 9:20. Surveying the park, she scanned the fountain. "Not today," she said out loud, patting her purse as if to say she wouldn't be wasting anymore pennies on wishes. Yesterday's wish still rested at the bottom with several other wishes surrounding its imperfect face. She worked her way to the pond and saw two nuns. Sister Anna Maria was there, and an older nun, who she assumed was Sister Magdalene Marie.

"Wow, ninety-one? She looks great," Madeline thought as she approached the nuns who had gently tossed one stone apiece into the water.

Sister Anna Maria turned after her silent prayer and smiled at Madeline. "Wow, you look different today."

"Ask and commit to him!" Madeline burst out in excitement.

The two nuns nodded as if they understood. Madeline fished out the piece of hard candy she had left in her pocket yesterday.

"Here, I didn't want to hurt your feelings, but I don't really like hard candy, and I know you love it, so I thought you might want it back."

The older nun turned and plucked it out of her hand. "Thank you," the old woman said. "These have been disappearing at a 'miraculous' rate the last few days from the convent." Her old gray eyes cutting toward the younger nun, who was now grimacing with guilt.

Madeline looked down at the basket of stones on the ground. She was ready to unburden her soul and ask forgiveness from a God and the unborn blue-eyed child she had never really known.

"Do you have any extra stones in there, and maybe an extra marker?"

CHARLOTTE, NORTH CAROLINA

"Coffee," Jerry said out loud as he shut off the engine to the black pick-up truck.

Jerry had a lot on his mind and a lot to sort through, but first he had to have his coffee to get his mind right. It was just after 6 a.m. and there were already a few customers inside the Chick-Fil-A. Even more snaked around the side for the drive-thru.

Pulling his sweatshirt over his head, he ambled through the parking lot. He coughed as the cold morning air filled his lungs. By noon, he probably wouldn't need the sweatshirt. That's how it worked this time of year.

He sighed as he saw the line in front of him. Jerry rubbed the graying stubble on his face and lamented that his belly expanded further over his waistband. Part of his mind wanted to inundate his thoughts with a list of things he had to do today. The tension was building, and he had been up most of the night. Coffee would help. Even with the caffeine, coffee would relax him.

The four-year-old with the runny nose in front of him stared at Jerry while clutching his mother's plump leg. She wasn't paying him any attention. She was too busy scrolling through a social media feed on her cell phone.

"Jesus," Jerry thought to himself. "If you weigh three hundred pounds, you shouldn't be out in public in tight black stretchy pants."

The woman turned back toward Jerry, and he wondered for a moment if he had said it out loud. "Who cares?" he thought, this time certain it was not out loud as the woman went back to her phone.

A couple of landscapers came in and filed in line behind him. Jerry liked it better when there were fewer people there. It was easier to concentrate, and he had a lot on his mind. The doctor told him that his lung cancer didn't have to be a death sentence, but Jerry knew he was too far gone, and he wasn't the kind of person to take care of himself. Even if he beat it this time, it would come back. It was only a matter of time.

Jerry had his bucket list of things to do, and nothing and nobody would stand in his way. He was going to live the rest of his life on his own terms, and everyone else would just have to get out of the way.

If only he could get through this line and get coffee.

The next person in line was slow to walk up to the counter. He, too, was busy with something on his cell phone. In fact, Jerry noticed that half the customers in the restaurant had their heads down, buried in their phones. Jerry imagined himself grabbing the man's cell phone, smashing it on the ground, telling him to get his head out of his ass and order his damn breakfast.

Jerry just shook his head. He did not own a cell phone anymore, nor did he want one. "What is wrong with everybody else?" Jerry wondered. He smiled at the thought of smashing the cell phone.

"Good morning, sir, and welcome to Chick-Fil-A," the thirty-something woman said from behind the register. That startled Jerry back to the present, and for a moment he felt sorry for her. She was a little pudgy and looked tired, even though she was cheerful. Jerry thought how much it must suck to work for minimum wage. "Will you be dining in this morning?"

Without thinking, Jerry heard himself rattle off his usual order, "Yes, I'd like the number one combo, and make it a large coffee, please.

"Oh, and leave room at the top for cream," he said before she could ask.

He handed her a ten, took his change and the placard with a number on it. He turned to face the dining room, and it was fuller than he had hoped. He grabbed a couple of tubs of half-and-half, and then finding a small empty table beside the door he had entered, he picked up one of the complimentary news-papers and sat down to wait for his breakfast. Seeing nothing that got his attention in the headlines, he placed the dollar bills into his wallet and accidentally dropped his change on the floor.

He paused as a customer walked right over his change, too busy to notice because his eyes were buried in his cell phone as well.

The floor was very clean, and he could smell the disinfec-tant as he bent down from his seat to pick up the change. He gained some pleasure in noticing he had a bicentennial quarter but seemed disappointed in the other coins which in-cluded a flawed penny with a scratch over Abraham Lincoln's nose. Another penny had a somewhat green hue to it.

Jerry slapped the change onto the table. He would leave it there as he didn't like having all the coins in his pocket. He sat up and was greeted by his server, holding a tray with his breakfast, and, of course, his coffee.

As the server left, Jerry smiled and unwrapped his chicken biscuit. The coffee was way too hot to drink right now. Jerry had scalded his tongue many times trying to ingest his coffee too soon, and that just always ruined the meal.

A police car pulled around the side of the restaurant, and Jerry cocked an eyebrow as he took a large bite of the biscuit. It didn't stop. Jerry looked back over at the black truck he had stolen two hours ago in Greensboro and wondered if it had already been reported. Surely not. Just in case, he'd probably need to find a new ride soon. That was an issue.

The Smith & Wesson M&P Shield 9mm handgun that he had stuffed in the back of his shorts was pressing hard on his tailbone. Jerry casually pulled it out, placed it on the table next to his meal, and covered it with the newspaper. Nobody seemed to notice. They were all staring at their phones.

"Still too many folks in here," Jerry thought to himself. "Probably not gonna get any less crowded, though."

He could see the steam rise from his coffee cup. Still too hot.

"Mountains or the beach," Jerry thought about where his next bucket list item would take him. He was never much of a beach guy, but he always wanted to go to one of those white sand beaches where you could actually see the bottom when you were waist-deep in the water.

The kid with the snotty nose waved as he walked by with his mother. He seemed happier now that his tummy was full. Jerry eyed the register, taking note of who seemed to be the manager on duty, and if there were any brave looking souls back there who might challenge him.

"Yeah, I can wait on a new ride after I get out of here," Jerry thought. "Just get what's in the registers and get out quick. Don't mess with the customers."

But first, he had to have his coffee.

BOSTON, MASSACHUSETTS

Dr. Abraham Weisman trudged up the stairs to his front door, wiped his feet, and was welcomed by the sweet smell of an apple pie baking in the oven. He took a deep breath and exhaled deeply; partly enjoying the smell and partly exhausted from a ten-hour day in his office.

"Long day?" his wife, Helen, asked. She saw the look in his seventy-eight-year-old eyes.

Helen knew better than to ask him why he didn't just retire from his psychiatric practice. He still loved it, was in great health, and could easily pass for sixty-five.

He didn't answer but smiled and rolled his eyes.

"You want to tell your grandson about it?" Helen asked rhetorically. "I'll bring dinner in there for you."

Abraham nodded, pecked Helen's cheek, and playfully asked, "Can I have the pie first?" He knew full-well that she wouldn't let him do that.

Abraham wouldn't talk to his wife about his cases. He took doctor-patient confidentiality seriously, but he found an outlet to relieve his own stress from the job by talking behind closed doors to his infant grandson, Abe. Just as he did for his patients during the day, having someone there to listen was therapeutic. Abe spent many nights there as his parents, including his mother, Abbey, worked odd schedules at the hospital.

Abraham sat in the rocking chair and watched his grandson wiggle in the crib. Helen followed a moment later and placed his meal and a piece of pie on the table next to him. The old man smiled at his wife, who left without a word and closed the door.

"Grandpa had a tough one today, Abe," Abraham said to his grandson.

Closing his eyes, he thought about his most troubling case and his first visit with Officer Frank Kelley. Abraham had an amazing memory that recalled every detail.

"Is this where I tell you about my childhood?" the tough-sounding officer said to the psychiatrist as he stood by the door, reluctant to come in.

Abraham smiled, having heard that and many other stereotypical jokes about his profession before. "Sure, if you want to. Or we can shrink your head, first."

Frank chuckled a little, closing the door behind him, but still uncomfortable about being ordered to see a psychiatrist. "I'm Frank Kelley, but I guess you know that already, right, Doc?"

"Yes, of course. I'm Doctor Abraham Weisman. You can call me Abraham or Doc if that makes you comfortable. Why don't you come on in and get settled," suggested Abraham, pointing to the matching brown couch and soft chair that were opposite where he was seated.

Frank had a tight grip on his service cap and hesitantly made his way to the seating area, thinking hard about whether to take the chair or the couch.

"Do I need to lay down?"

"Really, whatever makes you comfortable," Abraham said. "We're just going to talk. You can take your mask off if you'd like. I'll stay over here, and I've had the vaccine."

Frank stuffed the mask in his pocket and chose the couch

so he could spread out a little bit. He was a big man; a little over six feet tall and right at 200 pounds. "So, it's Abraham. Anyone call you Abe?" he asked.

"No," he replied with a smile, offering nothing else.

"OK. Weisman, eh? Like Wise man? I guess with a name like that, you couldn't help but be some kind of doctor," Frank said.

"I had a dentist whose last name was Warmflash," Abraham said. "No kidding!"

Frank was slightly more at ease but didn't like that his lieutenant made this necessary. He took in the doctor from head to toe: slender build, receding hairline on his dark brown head, khaki pants, red cardigan sweater, comfortable looking shoes.

"It's a German name; Weisman," Abraham continued and then noticing the confused look on the officer's face, he explained further. "I have an interesting family tree. But we're not here about my story, are we?"

"So, where do we start?" Frank asked.

"Tell me why you're here."

"Well, they told me I had to come, so here I am," Frank said. "I've been on the job for twenty years, and I ain't never done this."

"I know it can be uncomfortable," Abraham said.

"Look, I'm used to being uncomfortable," Frank said. "I wear a Kevlar vest, even in summer. It's hot. I carry a nightstick, radio, pepper spray, a flashlight, two sets of handcuffs, plus a couple of extra magazines for my service weapon. Chasing shitheads... I'm sorry, chasing alleged perpetrators..."

"You don't have to be politically correct here," Abraham interrupted, hoping it would make Frank more comfortable.

"I don't know. I guess haven't been sleeping much," Frank said as he rubbed his eyes. "I've just been tired, that's all."

Abraham didn't move in his chair but touched the eraser end of his pencil to his cheek. "Insomnia is not uncommon for law enforcement," Abraham said. "Honestly, you wouldn't be normal if parts of your job didn't keep you up at night.

"Let's talk about you first. Tell me where you're from, why you wanted to be a cop."

The two chatted pleasantly for the next fifteen minutes with the officer offering a little more into his life with each general question.

"I feel like we're on a date," Frank said with a laugh, then he straightened himself. "I mean with all the questions. Should I tell you about my mother?"

"If you want to. Maybe we can skip ahead," Abraham said.

Frank relaxed a little bit more on the couch as Abraham noticed his shoulders drop slightly, then the doctor continued, "Tell me about work."

"Work's OK, I guess," Frank said. "You know, the usual. Write some tickets. Get calls for domestic disputes. Sometimes there's a robbery." Frank stopped short while keeping eye contact with the doctor, seemingly omitting something.

"Anything out of the ordinary?" Abraham asked after a pause.

"I shot a guy," Frank said without emotion.

"First time?"

"No."

"Bad guy?"

"Yes."

"Did he die?"

"Yes."

"Was it justified?"

"Yes."

"Reporters all over you?"

"No."

"Why do you think that was?"

"The kid was white."

Abraham paused, which he could tell made Frank uncomfortable.

"Sorry, that was out of line," Frank said. "I just..."

"I understand," Abraham said. "These are challenging times. Everyone's been on edge.

"So, it was a kid? Tell me about it," Abraham continued as he shifted in his chair, keeping eye contact with the officer.

"Not much to tell," Frank said, turning his head to look out the window.

"Why'd you bring it up then?"

"Well, you asked," Frank said returning his gaze to the doctor.

"What did he do?"

"He and another guy knocked over a store, beat the clerk senseless," Frank said. "She was an old woman. Beat her bad."

"Go on. How did you catch up to them?"

"I got the 10-31 call on the radio. That's a crime in progress," Frank said, looking into his hands. "I was only a couple of blocks away. Another customer had run out of the store and called it in.

"So, I get there, and my backup arrives around the same time. The old lady was a mess. They knocked her down, and she hit her head and was bleeding all over the place. They took the money and whatever else they could grab. The eyewitness said they took a case of beer and some chips or some shit like that. Freaking amateurs. Still dangerous though. One of them had a gun, apparently. You get sensitive to the word gun. A gun changes anybody. A freakin' nobody suddenly becomes a player if he's got a gun."

Frank looked up and the doctor's expression didn't change, so he continued.

"So, my back-up is taking the report and EMS is there, so I ride out to canvass the neighborhood along with some other units. With the description we got, I figured these guys weren't going to be too hard to find. Probably a gang initiation."

"How long did it take until you found them?" Abraham asked, poking his cheek again with the end of his pencil.

"Ten minutes. Do you believe that? I'm riding out maybe three blocks out, and I see one guy wearing the Lakers hat and another guy wearing the red hoodie. Same description that we got from the eyewitness at the scene. So, I call for backup. There's about five of these guys hanging out shooting hoops and drinking beers. They see me rolling up, and they make a break for it. Two go one way, one guy another, and the three others, including my two guys, fly out in the same direction, so I punch it and start my pursuit."

"Still in your squad car?"

"Yeah. These dumbasses are running along the street, so I catch up to them in no time. They turn down an alley, so I block it with my cruiser and give backup my location. I know that unless one of these doors are unlocked, I've got them blocked in."

Abraham opened his eyes as his grandson gurgled and cooed for a moment. He smiled and took a forkful of his meatloaf before closing his eyes and recalling his next session with Officer Frank.

"Hello, Officer Kelley," Abraham said. "Come get comfortable."

Frank took his usual place on the couch.

"How have you been sleeping?" Abraham asked.

"About the same I guess," Frank said. "Some nights it's hard to sleep. I try drinking a couple of beers, but that makes me have to get up and piss in the middle of the night. Some nights I just wake up for no reason and can't go back."

Abraham sat in his usual chair, pencil in his hand. "Let's pick up where we left off last time. You told me you had tracked down the two thieves in the alley. One pulled a weapon, and you shot him. It sounds to me like you played it by the book. Still, that can be horrific for anyone, having to take a life."

"I know it," Frank said. "Look, none of us wants to shoot anybody. Like I told you last time, I've had to do it before, and it was justified. So, maybe that's not it. Maybe something else is keeping me up, I don't know."

After running through a series of questions about Frank's personal life and relationships at home and with co-workers, Abraham circled back. "Let's go back to the alley."

Frank repeated the scenario, and Abraham noticed it was nearly verbatim from his first account. "You seem to have all the details lined up, so let's take it slow."

Abraham opened his eyes to take another bite of dinner and ran through a couple more tedious sessions that bore no fruit. Frank didn't offer very much and would say he was doing better, but Abraham knew he was lying about that. The dark circles under his eyes told another story.

He closed his eyes again to recall today's session.

"So, how many more times do I need to come here?" Frank asked. "Can you just sign the form and tell my lieutenant that I'm good so I can get off desk duty?"

"I don't think you're there yet," Abraham said flatly. "We're going to try something different."

Abraham sat up in his chair and explained. "Close your eyes. I want you to take yourself out of the situation in the alley. You are watching it all on TV. So, you can play, fast forward, rewind, pause, or go frame by frame. Keep your eyes closed, no matter what I say. Do you understand?"

After acknowledging the idea, Frank took Abraham through the scene several more times at varying speeds. The script never changed until Abraham shouted, "Pause! Now take me through this part frame by frame."

"OK," Frank began again. "So, we're in the alley. I've called for backup, and I've drawn my weapon."

"Pause," Abraham said. "Why did you draw your weapon?"

"Because they committed a violent crime, and our witness at the scene said they had a gun."

"OK, frame by frame now. Where are the three guys, exactly."

"The one kid, who wasn't one of the guys reportedly at the store, is on the left facing me," Frank recalled with his eyes still closed. "White kid, skinny. Looked scared.

"The kid in the Lakers hat. Latino looking kid. He's to the right. Looks uneasy."

"And the one in the hoodie?" Abraham asked.

"He's in the middle. Back turned. Hands in front.

"I'm yelling, 'Hands in the air!'"

"Un-pause and go frame by frame," Abraham said.

"Lakers hat turns to hoodie. I still can't see hoodie's hands. He turns his right shoulder toward me and is pulling something out of the front of his pants. Lakers hat takes a step back. I train my gun on hoodie, I see the weapon. I fire three shots at center mass. He flies backwards. He's dead before he hits the ground."

Frank said nothing else but kept his eyes closed.

"What about the other two?" Abraham asked.

"They hit the deck and covered their heads."

"Then what?"

"I call in the 444 – officer involved shooting. Then I hear my backup coming down the street. I keep the other two on the ground with their hands on their heads."

"How old was the kid? The one you shot."

"Sixteen."

"That's tough."

"It was an air-soft."

"What's that?" Abraham asked, leaning back again.

"It's a like a BB gun, probably not as dangerous, but it looks freakin' real," Frank said defensively. "Jonny-D must have painted the orange tip at the end to make it look more real."

"Jonny-D?"

"Yeah. Sorry, Jonathan Davis was the kid's name."

"Why did you call him Jonny-D?"

Abraham opened his eyes, but still heard the sobs of Officer Frank in his office. He could hear Officer Frank shouting, "I never should have let him go! I should have made him mine."

Now it was Abraham who was hitting the pause button as he stood up from the rocking chair. He reached into the crib and cradled his grandson, Abe, holding him close and fighting back a tear.

"Yeah, your grandpa had a tough one today," he said as he kissed Abe gently on the forehead and placed him back down in the crib. He un-paused his session, only hearing Officer Frank's tearful confession of how he and his wife had fostered Jonny, whom he had always called Jonny-D around their house, for two years before he was adopted by another family at the age of seven. He relayed this to Abe to release the sorrow he felt for Frank, and for whatever had caused Jonny-D's life to take a wrong turn.

Abraham exhaled deeply as he whispered a prayer to his grandson while leaning over the crib. He spotted the familiar piggy bank on the shelf. He pulled the change from his pocket he received after stopping at Starbucks on his way to the office this morning.

An old, dirty penny lay on top of the other coins. He rubbed the chipped coin between his fingers. He was looking at the penny but speaking to the boy.

"I wonder where you will go," Abraham said, while dropping the penny into the bank. "I wonder where life will take you, and what you will see when you leave here. I hope you'll come back and tell me what your eyes have seen some day."

Abraham sat down again and ate his pie. It was still warm.

CPSIA information can be obtained
at www.ICGtesting.com
Printed in the USA
LVHW010340070722
722844LV00009B/543

9 781639 375660